Cosmic Collection #2

Don DeBon

Cosmic Collection #2

Don DeBon

First Printing
Copyright © 2016, 2017, 2018, 2022 Don DeBon

ISBN 978-1-948819-12-1
ISBN 978-1-948819-10-7 **(e-book)**

Contents

Cat Trouble

Chris sat frowning at the cat with it looking back at him with the same disdain. The cat had been a gift for his girlfriend. What a mistake that turned out to be. Now, he was stuck taking care of this hissing fur-ball.

Well, that wasn't entirely true. She didn't hiss at everyone else, only him. Try as he might, the cat wanted nothing to do with him. And now he was stuck alone with it for the next week while his girlfriend traveled to some European writer's conference.

"Well Fluffy, it is just you and me this week." The cat's eyes narrowed. Chris knew she didn't like the name Fluffy. Actually, she didn't like anything Chris called her, but Fluffy seemed to invoke a more negative reaction than the others by a small margin. In the end, he figured it didn't matter.

Chris extended a treat in his hand, but the cat took a swipe at him. Nails grazed, but didn't draw blood. "Geeze Fluffy! I was only trying to give you a treat."

A hiss came from the orange stripped tabby.

"Yeah, this is going to be a great week." Chris shrugged and left the apartment, feeling the sudden need to be anywhere else. An hour later stood in front of the wooden apartment door with two grocery bags filled with various cat treats and different brands of food. *There must be something here she will like.*

He turned the lock and entered. He put the bags on the kitchen counter and looked around. He didn't see Fluffy. The bowl of food he gave her earlier was untouched. He scraped the now dry food from the bowl, replaced it with a new expensive brand that looked better than what he ate last night for dinner, and put the bowl back on the floor.

"Fluffy? Where are you? I have some new food for you!" While he didn't expect the cat to come running –cats never did– he thought he would hear her stir somewhere in the apartment. After several minutes of silence, he decided perhaps other cat owners might know what to try next. He walked over to his laptop on the desk to find a large, gooey hairball in the middle of the keyboard. "Ugh! I'm going to kill that fur ball!" Chris took a long deep breath and forced himself to calm down. He could clean it up. For once, the extra expense of a hardened and waterproof laptop paid off.

Chris thought he heard something from the bedroom. He turned, took three steps, and pushed the door open. Fluffy ran past him in an eye-blink. "What's up with you?" Then he saw the reason. His side of the bed stood shredded; reduced to a mass of claw marks, stringy fabric, and feathers from his pillow. Some of which were still floating in the air. Wendy's side sat untouched.

Chris bit his tongue and counted to ten. When that wasn't enough, he counted to fifty. After doing this too many times to count, he didn't feel the need to rip Fluffy's head off. At least not that second. Turning, he left the bedroom and went back to the kitchen to get a garbage bag.

Chris opened the door under the sink, pulled out a bag, and

closed the door. He was about to walk back to the bedroom when he saw the little bowl of expensive cat food had been flipped over and shoved around like a hockey puck, leaving smears of food past the kitchen floor and onto the living room carpet. Red and brown streaks now dominated the otherwise white carpet.

Chris sighed and was thankful Wendy still wanted to keep separate apartments. While more expensive, right now he saw a definite advantage: once this week was over, he would never see Fluffy again. Wendy would come over here and leave that cat at her place. Or so he hoped.

Looking again at the Red and brown streaks across the carpet, he thought about calling animal control. The idea of paying them to house Fluffy for the week was tempting. But if Wendy ever found out, she would never forgive him.

Chris let out a deep sigh. "I guess I'm stuck," he muttered and headed back to the bedroom.

Hours later, the remnants of his bedding discarded, carpet cleaned, and his keyboard washed. It surprised him Fluffy didn't attack while he was cleaning. Instead, she watched him intently, moving from one mess to the other. No doubt planning her next assault.

Chris moved back to the kitchen, pulled out another can of different but still expensive cat food, and spooned it into a fresh bowl. He sat the bowl on the floor and pointed at it, then Fluffy. "There you are. And if you pull that same stunt again, I will let you starve. Perhaps that will change your mind!"

The cat sat on the edge of the couch, glaring at him. Her eyes narrowed and her tail twitched as if to say "Try it buddy!" She got down from the couch and casually walked over to stop in front of Chris. She sat down and continued her glare.

"Look, it is good food. The salesman said it was the best. And at that price, the can should be gold lined."

The cat continued her glare, never wavering for a second.

Chris stooped down and pointed at the bowl. "At least try it? How do you know if you don't even try?"

The cat stood up and took three steps towards the bowl. Lowered her head, took a sniff and sneezed. She knocked the bowl over with her right front paw and walked off.

"I think we are making progress. At least you didn't drag the bowl all over the living room carpet." Chris stood back up and saw Fluffy by the sliding glass door, watching a bird land on his balcony. "If you will eat pigeon, I will get that bird for you."

Fluffy looked at Chris, then her head swung back towards the bird.

"Yeah, I had better not. The neighbors might complain. And I have a hunch you would want me to end up in jail for shooting a pigeon for your dinner."

Fluffy remained unmoving, continuing to watch the bird with a fixed gaze. Her tongue slid out and licked both sides of her mouth as her eyes narrowed.

Chris cleaned out the food bowl again and filled it with another type that smelled like chicken. He placed the bowl by the cat. Fluffy looked at it, but her gaze swiveled back towards the bird still sitting on Chris' porch. He threw his hands in the air. "Fine! If you want to starve, that is fine by me!" He stormed off into his bedroom, refusing to watch the ornery cat any further.

* * *

Chris took a deep breath letting the smell of spring fill his nostrils as he walked back to his apartment. It had been over a day, and Fluffy still was not eating. He had managed to get her to drink a little, although more water got on him than in the cat.

Walking past an alley, he heard what sounded like Fluffy's hiss, followed by something a lot larger. "Can't be Fluffy, I left her back in the apartment. Still, I had better check this out." Chris turned and entered the space between the two buildings. Back behind a dumpster, he found a cat backed into a corner. The red collar with the bow proved it was Fluffy, and she was in trouble. Two feet away sat the largest cat Chris had ever seen. One eye sported an old deep gash above it. The larger animal made another hiss that sounded like a combination of a German shepherd's growl and a bobcat. Most dogs, even larger ones, would run from this creature. If there was such a thing as Catzilla, this was it.

Catzilla gave an even louder, deep rumbling hiss. If Chris didn't know better, he would have thought something five times its size made the sound. The fur all over Catzilla rose, and a paw raised with claws extended.

"Hey you! Leave my cat alone!" Chris yelled. He grabbed a pipe that lay near the dumpster and banged it on the capacious green container.

Catzilla's head whipped around to face Chris, giving Fluffy enough time to dart past and hide behind Chris. Catzilla hissed again, his fur raised even higher as he took two steps towards them.

Chris saw a bottle of liquid sticking out of the dumpster. He grabbed it, tossed it into the air, and hit it with the pipe in his other hand. The bottle soared past Catzilla impacting the brick wall above and behind him. The compromised plastic exploded, causing its liquid contents to rain down, covering Catzilla, drenching him. He sneezed several times, moaned, and took off toward the other end of the alley.

A noxious odor wafted to Chris' nose, and he knew why. Spoiled lemon juice. No wonder Catzilla ran. He dropped the pipe and his eyes drifted down to Fluffy sitting at his feet. "You okay?" Fluffy jumped into his arms. Chris stroked the cat. "Guess you are. And you are welcome. Come on, let's go home."

Chris fumbled, trying to get the keys out of his pocket while holding Fluffy. "You know this would be easier if you were on the floor." Fluffy looked at him with wide eyes. "Okay, I won't. But you will have to get down sometime."

A voice reached out from behind. "Chris! I see you found your cat!"

Chris turned to see Mrs. Bingley standing in her usual oversized dress that did nothing to disguise her large frame. "Hello Mrs. Bingley. How did you know she was lost?"

Mrs. Bingley's eyes drifted down. "I'm afraid that is my fault. I heard something odd, and I used the key you gave me. But when I opened the door, a cat shot past me and into the hall. I looked, but couldn't find her. I tried your cell, but only went to voice mail."

"Yeah, sorry about that. I forgot to charge it last night and left it home."

"It is I who should be sorry. I couldn't forgive myself if something happened to your cat because of what I did." Mrs. Bingley took a step closer and reached out to stroke Fluffy's fur. The cat purred in a deep, rhythmical fashion. "Especially since she is such a sweetheart."

Chris looked down at the purring cat in his arms. *She wasn't an hour ago.* He turned his gaze back to Mrs. Bingley and smiled. "No harm done. Thanks for checking."

Mrs. Bingley gave one last stroke along the cat's back and smiled. "Of course. What are neighbors for?" She turned and headed back towards her apartment.

Chris got the door open to reveal why Mrs. Bingley had come over in the first place. Several potted floor plants were tipped over, spilling dirt all over the carpet. The huge mess stretched far into the kitchen. He looked down at Fluffy. "You aren't going to be doing things like this again, are you?" The cat gave her head a quick shake. "Good."

* * *

Keys clinked as the locked turned and Wendy appeared in the doorway. She entered, wheeling a large luggage bag behind her. "Ugh, what a long trip."

Chris sat in his favorite chair watching the big screen TV on the wall. Fluffy looked up from the curled position in his lap, but didn't stop purring. "Hey Sweetheart, I thought you were going to drop by your apartment first?"

Wendy looked through jet-lagged eyes. "I know, but yours is closer. I really need a shower and bed. I hope you don't mind."

Chris smiled. "Of course not."

Wendy's eyes drifted down to the cat in Chris' lap and back up. "Well, I see you two worked things out. I knew you only needed a few days alone with her."

Chris looked down at Fluffy. "Do think we should tell her or not?"

Fluffy turned her head back towards Chris, whipped it back

to look at Linda, and shook her head three times in quick succession.

"Nope, didn't think so."

Fluffy's eyes narrowed, then flashed. *"Xeon Agent 3241 here, report 446. These humans may be worth saving after all."*

Scared Stiff

Click

Melanie shuddered as the almost inaudible sound from Roy's EMG353 as he clicked off the safety still sent chills down her spine. What if they heard?

Roy looked over at the gorgeous researcher sitting on the floor next to him. Melanie had the curves of a supermodel, and almost nothing was hidden in the short nightdress she was wearing. For a researcher, she just didn't fit the part. He crouched down further. Ready.

Hisssss

Around the corner, just down the corridor, Roy heard him again. A Pinatron warrior. Carefully snaking a little peep camera smaller than a finger around the corner, an image flashed into the heads up display in his helmet. The alien had removed his helmet. They never remove their helmets! Roy could see the bald head, pointed ears, simple slits for a nose and razor-sharp teeth as the alien sneered and sniffed the air.

Roy knew the only reason a Pinatron would dare remove the helmet to his bio armor was if it was certain no one would live to tell the tale. His muscles twitched as the alien took another step, making a faint clink on the deckplate as one of his toe talons touched.

Melanie shivered at the sound. It was getting closer, much closer. And this space marine didn't get out and shoot it. What was he waiting for? She sucked in a breath and held the chemical touched air, remembering how this research station was supposed to be far beyond the front lines of the war. Pinatron's shouldn't be here. Heck, this place hadn't even been operational for more than a day. She was the first researcher to arrive. The rest of the team wasn't due for several weeks.

She silently cursed the SpaceGov and their attempt at efficiency. All the technicians left as soon as she arrived, saying everything was automated and she didn't need them. The techs had another station to set up. Yeah right, another station. What about *this* one! They had paid for it, after all.

All was going well, although it was a little lonely. Melanie had dealt with that before. And the rest of the team would arrive soon. One advantage she didn't mind: being able to take the largest quarters. She didn't have much, the warp transport had little room for her luggage, not that she carried much these days. She barely had the clothes on her back, with the rest of her cargo weight allocated to special equipment and data storage modules.

That night though, looking at her empty walls and closet, she gave into a whim and had the fabricator build something special to sleep in. Perhaps a bit frivolous but darn it she was tired of sleeping in the same bulky, itchy one piece, standard issue sleep suit. Thankfully, she still had the design in one of her personal data cores. If the team was there, she would never have done it, but tonight it was only her. Why not?

She was sleeping soundly when a hand reached out and covered her mouth. "Shh, I am not going to harm you. My name is Roy. I am here to protect you. The station has been compromised. I need to get you out of here."

Melanie laid with her eyes wide. The man had flipped up his helmet of his armor, revealing a battle worn face. "I . . . I . . . compromised?" she whispered.

"Yes, Pinatrons!" Roy said quietly.

"How?"

"I don't know. Did you have your defensive systems up?"

"I think so. Or they should have been. I don't know, the techs left in a big hurry. It is possible that it wasn't activated."

"The techs left? Are you the only one here? What's your name anyway?"

Melanie nodded somberly as she pulled the sheet further up. "Yes. I am the first to arrive. The rest of the team is not due for several weeks. My name is Melanie."

"Great, that explains why I didn't see anyone else."

"How did you find me?"

"This is the Station Manager's quarters. I figured if there was anyone aboard, I should find them here this time of night."

"And where are the Pinatron's?"

Roy's helmet flipped down and a moment later, it opened again. "Lower levels. They seem to be looking for something. But they are moving fast and will be here soon. Let's go!"

"But I'm not dressed! Let me get dressed first!"

"There is no time. Besides, those standard issue sleep suits are fine."

"Umm . . . I'm . . . not wearing one."

Roy's eyes went wide. "You are naked?"

"No! But I'm not dressed either."

"So you are wearing a sleep suit, big deal," Roy said with a shrug.

"No, I told you I'm not wearing one," Melanie said as her cheeks defied her and grew bright red.

"Well whatever, you are wearing something. We don't have time for you to change." Roy said as his helmet lowered and he checking his scanner display again. "I detect a life form just down the other corridor. If we don't leave right now, he will see us and all bets are off. You know how deadly they are. And it is just me here. You are just lucky I happened to be in the area and spotted the Pinatron ship using its breaching tube on the lower levels. Now get out of that bed! We are going now!" Roy said as he pulled the cover off of the bed and was suddenly thankful his helmet was down concealing his open mouth. For there was something he never thought he would see, certainly not out here. A woman wearing a very sexy piece of lingerie. Loose fitting, in some areas and tighter in others. It more resembled a short mini dress with lace edges around her breasts held up with spaghetti straps. The purple satin shimmered slightly as she moved. His jaw snapped shut when he realized it was still hanging open.

Melanie's eyes widened, then shrank as she tried to cover herself. "Okay, now you know."

"Where in the world did you get that out here?" Roy's voice came through his helmet speaker.

"Never mind, just let me grab something."

"I told you, no time!" He said, grabbing her wrist, and they ran out of her quarters and into the corridor.

They had just passed the threshold of her quarters when Roy raised a hand, one finger outstretched next to his helmet. He made a motion towards his unseen nose. Crouching down, he put his back to the wall and motioned for her to do the same. The Pinatron was here.

Hisssss

The retched sound snapped Melanie out of her memories. She looked up at Roy, his face hidden behind his helmet. She cursed the purple lingerie and wanting one night in something other than the annoying sleep suit. Then this guy shows up in her quarters and sees her in it. She always hoped that if a man saw her in it, it was her boyfriend, not some total stranger.

Roy looked back, popped his helmet open and mouthed, "stay here and be quiet." His helmet lowered and glowed slightly. He checked his EMG353 and wished he had brought an energy cannon instead. But he thought he would get out of here long before now. This was supposed to be a simple extraction. He sucked in a breath and held it as he tried to think through his options.

The Pinatron took another step, its talon scratching the deck plate. It hissed again. Roy knew it could smell them. Their sense of smell was almost as accurate as human sensors. But it wouldn't know exactly where they were, and he could use this to his advantage.

Melanie shook, and Roy reached back to quiet her.

* * *

Melanie tapped several keys and the formula on her screen changed and shifted as the simulation ran. The math seemed sound, and the simulations all said the same thing. But the trials had shown otherwise. She frowned and sat back, rubbing her face. She glanced at the timepiece on her wrist and realized she had been working at this straight for six hours.

Her eyes drifted around the small quarters. While large areas were never something she craved, these quarters were micro compared to others she had in the past. A desk, terminal, bed, fresher in the corner, and a locker at the foot of the bed for personal items. And she could touch her bed with her foot while at her desk. Still though, she didn't mind. She wasn't here except for working or sleeping. And if she ever wanted more space, there was always the lab.

She and the team were at the *Gemini* station working on a better energy utilization curve that could pull every gigawatt from Klarni Crystals almost instantly, giving a ship far more range and speed. The problem: while the theory was sound, practice turned out to be more problematic. They had already lost three ships with the enhanced drives. The drives always worked fine, until they didn't. No one could find out why. One ship, the *Polaris* disappeared without a trace and hadn't even engaged the enhanced drive.

The *Reclaon* had observed a flash towards the AFT section, near the main engines a second before arcs of energy fanned out from the section dancing all over the hull. Three seconds later, the *Polaris* disappeared. SpaceGov first thought the report had to be fake, but the *Reclaon* had recorded the entire incident.

To make matters worse, the *Polaris* never responded to the *Reclaon's* repeated hails once the first flash was seen. No one knew if they were dead from that point on, or a loss of power made them unable to respond. Captain Arno said he thought he saw lights aboard the *Polaris* during the incident, proving they had power. But the investigation proved inconclusive. It could have been the energy eruption from the AFT section, causing the lights Arno saw to illuminate. When Arno disagreed, the investigation board declared their communications system must have been damaged at the time of the overload.

Captain Arno knew better than to press the matter further.

Melanie leaned forward, tapping another key as the simulation continued to twist and warp. Her stomach rumbled, but she tried to put it out of her mind. *I will eat after this simulation is done.*

The door to her quarters pinged. Melanie sighed at the brief chime and sat back again, looking down. She still had on last night's sleep suit. Although she didn't get much sleep last night. Formuli kept racing through her mind, and she figured she could sleep later, getting up to work on them.

Melanie hated how these generic sleep suits fit. Or lack of it. They draped over her body and hid, rather than showed, every curve she had. She thought about taking off the ugly, bulky, unflattering, plain blue overalls, put on something more day-wear, and throw these in the fresher. But decided it would take too long. Whoever was at the door wouldn't wait much longer before asking security for a door override. And wearing last-nights sleep suit when the door opened was better than being caught naked while putting on something else. She sighed again, swallowed, and took a deep breath. "Yes?"

"Mel? It's Sofia, open up," came from the speaker embedded into the door's control panel on the right.

Melanie dropped her head for a second, stood up, turned around, and waved her hand over the door's control panel. The quick wave allowed the system to scan her hand and unlocked the door. She tapped another button and the double door parted down the middle with a bit of a grind at the end. *I need to have maintenance look at that.*

Melanie's eyes fell upon Sofia Bock, the team's so-called leader. While she didn't have the title officially, but since everyone else didn't want to send in reports, and Sofia tolerated it, they let her fill the role when those from SpaceGov wanted an update or other paperwork. She stood in her white lab coat, but Melanie could see she was wearing dress pants and a shirt under it. *Great, she needs something.* "Mel? Can I have a word?"

Melanie stood aside and waved her in while pressing the button on the door to close it as soon as she crossed the threshold. "What is it? I'm in the middle of something."

Sofia eyed Melanie's sleep suit. "So I see. Did you know it is after 09:00?"

Melanie rolled her eyes. "Of course I know. But I'm in the middle of something and I can do just as much work here as in the lab. Well, more because I don't have people bugging me every five minutes."

Sofia's eyes narrowed. "We don't bug you. If you haven't noticed, we leave you alone."

Melanie sighed and plopped down in her desk chair, pulled her knees up to her chest, and pointed to the unmade bed. "Sorry, I didn't have a good night last night."

Sofia nodded. "I can tell." She frowned, looking at the small metal bunk cot. "No thanks, I will stand if you don't mind."

Melanie gave a half-hearted shrug. "Fine with me. So, what's up? Or were you bugged I wasn't in the lab?"

Sofia grinned. "No, we don't care if you are there or here. You know that. Even if we don't see you, we can see your activity. It is the best work of the team."

Melanie felt the heat raise in her cheeks despite herself. "Thank you. And now I know you want something or you wouldn't be trying to butter me up."

Sofia chuckled. "I'm not trying to butter you up. But I did want to tell you we decided to move off of *Gemini*."

Melanie blinked. This was the first time she had heard of this. "Leave *Gemini?* Why? Everything is right here."

Sofia sighed, parting her white lab coat, and sat on the edge of the bed anyway. "I think you know. We don't have a single instance of data on what happened aboard the ships we lost with the new drives."

Melanie raised a finger. "We do have data. We know there was a power surge of some sort, at least on the *Polaris.*"

Sofia let out a breath and shook her head. "Yes we do. But that observation is questionable."

"How is it questionable? He is a reputable captain and there are recordings to back up everything he said."

"I know, I know. But you haven't been in contact with SpaceGov like I have. There are suspicions he forged that video and destroyed the ship himself."

"What? That's impossible! There would be evidence if he–"

Sofia raised her hand, palm out. "I know. And I agree with you. But it doesn't matter what we think. SpaceGov wants to see progress, and we don't have any to offer."

Melanie sat forward, her bare feet shuffled across the slick, cold floor. "What are they doing? Canceling our project?"

"No, not yet. But I can see it is only a matter of time. Which is why I and the rest of the team think we need to progress to the next phase."

Melanie cocked her head. "The next phase? How can we do that when the data is inconclusive?"

"Not safely, I assure you."

Melanie sat back, pulled her feet back from the cold floor, and tucked them under her. "That's why you want to leave *Gemini?* So we can do experiments without risking everyone on this station?"

Sofia nodded. "Yes, we always knew we would have to move at some point. Just not so soon."

Melanie closed her eyes and opened them with deliberate slowness. "Okay, when do we leave?"

Sofia shook her head. "Not us, you."

"What? I don't understand?"

"I have procured a new site where we can do our research in complete privacy. You are to go on ahead and take all the vital data with you. It is one of the newest stations, LW-32. It should be done by the time you arrive."

"A LW station? Are you kidding?" While Melanie never heard the actual designation, everyone said it stood for a long way out. "And what do you mean it should be done by the time I arrive?"

"It is still under construction, but I was in communication with the build crew and it will be done by the time you get there."

Melanie blinked. "But why only me?"

"We know the isolation won't bother you. The rest of us would go crazy being alone for a few weeks."

Melanie had to agree. She did work better in isolation, even though she got along with other people fine ... usually. "Okay, I will give you that, but why don't we all go at once?"

"Because someone has to be there when the station goes operational. The build crew won't stay aboard after that point. And I could only secure transport for one of us right now. The rest will arrive three weeks later. We will send the latest data core and prototype with you. Heck, you might even find the solution before we get there."

Melanie inched herself out of the chair, the cheap fabric of the sleep suit making rustling sounds as she stood. She closed her eyes and opened them slowly, focusing on Sofia. She licked her lips. "When do I leave?"

"The transport arrives within the hour. It cost us a good portion of our reserve to get you out there this fast, but we would lose the station to someone else if we didn't. The data core and prototype are packed and ready. All we need is to get you and them aboard."

"All right, give me a few minutes to hop in the sonic, change, pack, and I'll be ready." Melanie pressed a spot on the door control, and the door slid open.

Sofia smiled. "Thank you. We will be right behind you, don't worry," she said, stepping into the hallway. The door shut a second later.

Melanie rolled her eyes as the door locked. "More like three weeks behind."

* * *

Melanie sat back in her seat and shifted her weight as the starliner *Serenity* nestled up against the docking port at the base of LW-32. It surprised her being the only one aboard not staff, a special trip like this must have cost a fortune. No wonder Sofia was so adamant about her not to miss it. Not like she would, anyway.

While the *Serenity* was a starliner, she was not much on comforts. Speed, yes, but comfort was certainly lacking. Other than her seat, and eight others like it, there wasn't anywhere for her to go. Unlike most starliners with full cabins and recreational facilities, this one only had upright seats. Comfortable yes, but they couldn't compare to a bed or working out in a full gym with an actual water pool. The only benefit, being the single passenger, she had more room than usual, and she could stretch out in the seats. But by the time they reached the station, what she would have given for a bed. Even the hard metal-framed cot back in her quarters on *Gemni* station looked inviting.

Melanie sat in the padded seat, tapping on the console controls next to her right hand embedded in the arm of the chair. The smooth fabric of her red blouse made a slight rustling sound on the seat's fabric as she continued to tap the controls. Sighing, not finding anything worth watching, she smoothed the black skirt that ended just above her knees and crossed her legs, letting the matching black shoed foot dangle back and forth.

She looked over her shoulder at one of the stewardesses. Tall with black hair, dressed in the standard blue uniform with white trim the line had, she smiled with a gleam in her eye. She turned and when her eyes met Melanie's; the smile grew. The stewardess took several steps closer, her low-heeled dress shoes making muted noises on the carpet, and leaned over. "Can I help you with something, my dear? Would you like a cocktail, or perhaps one of our dinner bars?" She gestured towards the small hidden room nestled in the back of the cabin area. "I can get you one, and they do taste better than they look. Trust me."

Melanie tried to hide her discomfort. Dinner bars were the same everywhere. Edible, but that was about it. Not to mention drier than a desert planet. Last time she had one, she could have sworn she drank a gallon of water afterwards. While she was hungry, a dinner bar was the last thing she wanted to eat. She shook her head, her long hair waving back and forth. "No, thank you. I was just wondering how long until we can disembark?"

The stewardess' smile grew even more, and Melanie

wondered how. "I don't know, but considering you are the only passenger, it shouldn't be more than forty minutes."

Melanie blinked. "Forty minutes? I thought I saw the ship dock several minutes ago?" She pointed to one of the small view ports on the other side of the ship.

The stewardess nodded. "We did, but you know regulations. We must file we arrived, and the station technicians need to certify our connection is stable. Once that is done, they will give us, I mean you, clearance to disembark."

Melanie nodded. "Oh I know about regulations, but I thought all of that was taken care of by Sofia?"

The stewardess' one shoulder lifted, then dropped. "I don't know. But this is standard procedure. We haven't been told we could skip the usual protocol."

Melanie sat back in her chair, her fingers drumming the side of the console mounted in part of the right arm of the seat. "Okay, I waited this long for a real bed and something decent to eat. I suppose I can wait another forty minutes."

The stewardess nodded. "Of course, if you need anything else, just let me know."

Melanie watched as the Stewardess walked past her towards the hidden staff compartment in the back. *What I need is something other than a dinner bar. I'm hungry enough to start eating this seat soon. But I suppose I can last another few minutes.*

Twenty minutes later, the captain's voice came over the speakers hidden in the ceiling. "To our passengers, we have now docked at station LW-32 and have been given clearance for disembarkation. Thank you for flying with us."

Melanie rolled her eyes as she stood up and tried to work the kicks out of her back. *Next time, I'm telling Sofia to get someone else if the liner doesn't have better accommodations.* She was glad to have brought several synth-meat sandwiches. They were a lot better than the liner's dinner bars. But she ate the last one six hours ago.

Melanie stretched again in the middle aisle and several pops could be heard from her back. She flicked her long black hair over her shoulder, reached up, slipped her keycard into the slot in the cargo compartment above her to unlock it. The red light to the right of the slot changed to green, and she could hear a slight thunk as the locks disengaged. Melanie couldn't fault them for security, but then again, Sofia never would have used them otherwise.

She pushed open the compartment and pulled down the two large hard-sided cases, one at a time, setting them into the aisle. The first case held her clothes and a few personal data cores. The second had the prototype Klarni Crystal Reactor Core. There was more equipment in the lower hold but, these were the most important ones. She grabbed the two cases by their handles and made her way towards the back.

The stewardess stepped out from the back compartment and into the aisle as Melanie approached. She pointed to the two cases. "Do you need help with those?"

Melanie shook her head. "No, I've got these. But if you could make sure they transfer the rest of the equipment from the lower hold, I would appreciate it."

The stewardess smiled again. "Of course, and thank you for flying with us."

If I didn't know better, I would swear they were all androids. I could have had better conversations with a trained dog. Must be something in the training to keep all passengers beyond arm's length.

* * *

Melanie stepped off the main docking tube into the airlock at the base LW-32. The larger, long-term stations like *Gemini* often looked like a giant spinning ball in space. LW stations were more spider-like, with different sections branching off the central core. Not as easy to get around, or live in, but they were fast to assemble in comparison.

The air lock stayed open, as they usually did for a liner docking, although it would likely be closed right after her. The large green lights above the door indicated the hard-seal with several redundant systems were intact. Which, of course, if it was anything else, every alarm in the station would likely go off. Not to mention all doors would close and seal as a precaution.

She walked through the airlock onto the station itself. The polished metal floors looked better than she expected, and the air smelled fresh. Another sign this station hadn't been operational long. After a while, it would have a more mechanical and slightly greasy smell once the recycling system had been operational for several more months.

Melanie stood at the entrance, looking up and down the rounded corridor and at the lack of anyone to greet her. Usually, someone would greet the passengers from a liner, or any other docking, for that matter. Yet she didn't see a soul. She took a few more steps on the polished floors. She expected them to be slippery, but her shoes didn't slide at all, even when she tried. She took a slight bouncing step to test the gravity, and it seemed normal. For several minutes she wondered what to do, then she noticed a console interface on the far wall, half-way down the corridor near a lift tube.

She walked down the corridor, placed the cases on the floor

on either side of her, and placed her hand on a control panel. The screen lit up, recognizing her, and listed several options. She asked for a map and the screen displayed a blueprint of the station and its many levels. She was about to ask where everyone was when the tube door to her right opened. A man in technician's white overalls with red trim stepped out. He didn't seem to even notice her and walked right past. The smell of fresh exertion wafted from him, causing Melanie to wince as he hurried heading down the corridor and towards the *Serenity's* air lock.

"Hey!" she said, reaching out. "What's going on?" The man continued on, not seeming to hear her. She raised two fingers to either corner of her mouth and blew as hard as she could. A shrill, deafening whistle rocketed out, bouncing over the corridor's smooth, rounded walls.

The man stopped in his tracks and turned around and rubbed his ears. "Ouch! Don't do that! What's your problem?"

Melanie blinked. "My problem? How about yours? What's the rush? And why wasn't there anyone to great me when I came aboard?"

The man started walking backward, lifting one shoulder then letting it fall. "I don't know. I'm not in charge of that. But I was told to get some equipment moved up to the lab level as quickly as possible and prep for the liner's departure. We're all leaving soon."

Melanie blinked. "Leaving? How? There isn't another ship docked here."

The man nodded. "No, but there is one on the way and it should arrive in a few hours."

Melanie scrunched up one eye as she cocked her head. Sofia had said they would leave after getting the station operational, but she didn't think it would be this quick. "That soon? Why the rush?"

"We have another station to get online, and we're already behind schedule. Now, if you will excuse me." The man turned on his heel and ran, disappearing into the airlock before Melanie could say anything more.

* * *

Melanie stepped into the lift tube carrying the two hard-sided cases and tapped the control with her knuckle for the lab deck, the highest one on the station. The doors slid shut almost without a sound, and she felt the tube moving upwards. *The first thing to do is find someone who could answer more of her questions.* She knew little about this station layout except the main docking area was at the bottom and the lab area at the top. She hoped someone was up there she could talk to. She still couldn't believe no one was there to greet her when she arrived.

Melanie felt the tube slow, and the doors parted to another rounded corridor. She stepped out, and the doors slid closed behind her. Looking up and down the corridor, she saw the reinforced lab door a few yards to the left. To the right, scattered along the corridor walls were doors with signs above them indicating different storage areas. The Klarni Core's weight pulled at her right hand, and she thought about putting it in one of the storage rooms, but decided to wait until she could talk with someone in charge.

She turned, taking a deep breath of newly recycled air, and turned to the left, heading down the smooth metal floor. After several steps, she reached the reinforced lab door, set down the case in her right hand, and placed her palm on the reader to the right of the door. The black square, slightly twice the size of her hand, lit up as a single bar of light started from the top and raced down towards the bottom, scanning. A few seconds later the small screen above it flashed "Access Granted" in large green type, and she heard heavy bolts along the sides and top of the door retract into the walls and floor. A second later, the door split into in a Z pattern and retracted into the walls on either side.

The security system was certainly stronger here than on *Gemini*.

She took a step inside to total pandemonium. People were running everywhere. She counted at least twenty-five she could see with ease. All wearing technician jumpsuits. The lab main was easily the largest she had seen on a station, and she had a tough time seeing the other side of it with the various systems being installed and people crawling all over them.

Off towards the left, she saw a man with a data tab pointing as he started to shout. "Come on people! This should have all been done yesterday. And the first researcher is aboard. What are you trying to do? Make me look bad?"

There was a chorus of laughter as they continued working. Melanie figured they must be almost finished in here as she saw several of the technicians closing panels and sealing them with high-torque power drivers. She walked over to the man that had shouted. He wore the standard technician jumpsuit, but he had more rank pins along the edges and gold trim along his shoulders. She took another deep breath and tried to fight off the shiver that was going up her spine as she gave him her best smile. "Hello, I'm Melanie Phelps. Where do I put this?" She held up the case containing the Klarni Core.

The man's eyes went wide for a second before he regained

his composure. Clearly, he wasn't expecting her up here so soon. "Oh, hello, I'm sorry. I wasn't expecting you to be up in the lab yet. As you can see, we are almost done, but not quite ready for you. The living quarters are a couple of decks below us. Just pick one, get situated, and we should be done by then."

Melanie pointed back towards the main lab's doors with the case in her left hand. "I saw several storage rooms on my way here. Could I put it in one of those? I don't really want to take it to my quarters. It is heavy, and I'm sure the quarters are short on space as it is."

The man cracked a smile. "So sure, are you of that? Well, I suppose you can use the storage lockers. They are finished. But please activate the security systems afterwards. We haven't yet."

She wanted to ask more questions, but the Klarni Core felt like it was gaining ten pounds every minute. Her arm burned and felt as if it was going to fall out of the socket. Melanie nodded at the man and turned to leave. The door, recognizing her leaving, split into its Z shape, and she walked through with it sealing right behind her.

She sighed and continued down the rounded corridor with its brushed metal paneling towards the storage rooms. She stopped at the door of the first one and started to lower the case containing the Klarni Core to the floor and unlock the door when it opened without her authorization. Her eyes widened for a split-second before she remembered the lead technician said they hadn't activated the security in these rooms yet. Green lights lit up on the control panel and the door split down the middle, retracting into the walls.

Melanie peered inside. The room wasn't very large, but the walls were lined with multiple empty metal racks and one large center rack that split the room down the middle. She went to one of the closest racks, placed the case on it, and left the room. The doors closed behind her, and she placed her hand upon the black scanning plate next to the doors. A bright line again scanned her palm and the display above lit up with options. She engaged the security and set it to the highest level, with access only granted to herself or Sofia. Sighing, she rotated her arm and heard several pops as she rubbed her shoulder. Glad the core was safe, she walked back towards the lift and to the quarters below.

* * *

Melanie entered the room at the end of the corridor. The door split, revealing a room easily ten times the size of the one she had on *Gemini* station. She almost picked the first quarters she came to, but then her feet carried her down to this one. She stepped within and the doors whisked shut behind her. The recessed panels grew in intensity, lighting the entire area. Off to her right sat a full kitchen and to the left a desk several times the one she had on *Gemini* sat with a terminal lit up displaying the name LW-32. A large bed sat almost out of sight in a separate, actual bedroom area.

Melanie almost turned around, thinking the suite of rooms was too much for her. Then she decided she deserved to have a decent sized room for a while. Sofia might complain when she got here, but then she should have come instead. Melanie entered the bedroom and placed her case on the bed. She popped the latches, and the case opened to reveal a standard sleep suit, another change of clothes, a set of dress pants, shirt, and a pair of classic closed toe black heels similar in style to what she was wearing now. Except she had decided to wear flats on this trip.

Melanie sighed at her meager belongings. She reached into a flap behind the clothes on the top section and pulled out one of her personal data cores. She looked at the square chip in her hand with its edge connector and folded her hand around it. Inside contained most of her personal files, including clothing templates. She may not have brought much, but she could create more, and right now, she wanted to. First thing though, was to attack the kitchen.

The door pinged, and she slipped the data core into a small pocket on her skirt as she turned around. "Yes?" she said.

The door split, revealing the lead technician she spoke to earlier. He stood there for several seconds, looking at her. "I didn't know you were the station manager?"

Melanie blinked. "Station manager?"

"Yes, these quarters are reserved for the station manager. You didn't know?"

Melanie shrugged. She had a hunch when she saw the size, but now she didn't care. "No, I didn't. But since I am the only one here of the team, it doesn't matter much."

The man cracked a grin large enough to swallow a horse. "If you say so. I wanted to let you know the lab is completed, and we are placing the finishing touches on the station. A ship will arrive for us within the hour, and we will be out of your hair."

Melanie blinked. While the guy she first spoke to after she arrived had mentioned the ship arriving, she thought he must have been mistaken on its projected arrival. "So soon? From what I saw, I thought you had a lot more to do yet."

The man shook his head. "Nope, we are done and have another station to build. I have taken the liberty of keying all the systems over to you. You now have full access to the entire station. I assume you know how to run it?"

Melanie took a diminished step forward as she looked down. "Not exactly. I have never been aboard a LW station before. I know of them, but not all the details. I had expected to have you show me before you left."

The man sighed. "I'm sorry, but as I said, we have a tight schedule to keep. I have to assume you have done some administration before or you wouldn't have been sent on ahead. It isn't much different and if you have problems, there are help files built into the system."

Melanie frowned. Did this man really think she was clueless? While she may not have had experience with this kind of station before, and would have preferred instruction, especially from the good-looking man standing in front of her, but she didn't want him to know that. The systems were standardized and almost all the same anyway. "Of course, don't worry about it. I have dealt with these kinds of systems before." While not entirely true, most of the staff aboard *Gemini* took care of such systems, and they were mostly automated anyway. The last thing she wanted was for this man to think of her as some helpless female when she was anything but.

The man smiled. "Good, then we will get out of your hair." And he left before Melanie could say anything more.

* * *

Melanie watched from the airlock window the boxy cargo ship with all the technicians aboard, disconnect from the station. She sighed as it activated several small docking thrusters, backing away from the airlock before using lateral thrusters to rotate away from the station. A moment later, their main engines glowed to life. A few seconds after that, she saw a slight flash as the ship engaged the full drive and launched out of her vision.

She sucked on another blub of water as she turned away from the airlock and headed back towards the lift and her quarters above. While the last thing in the world she wanted to eat was a dinner bar, it was the only thing the kitchen had ready-to-eat, and she didn't want to take a chance of missing the technicians leaving on the off-chance they needed to tell her something they forgot earlier.

But no such luck.

Instead, her mouth felt like a sand pile for no reason. Melanie shook her head and stepped into the lift tube, rocketing up towards her quarters on deck four. She stepped out and walked towards her quarters, thinking about all the different things she could make to try to remove the dinner bar aftertaste from her mouth.

Less than an hour later, she relished in synth-pasta, meatballs, and had even made a loaf of bread. Thankfully, the kitchen had the latest equipment. It didn't take her near as long as she expected. Which was good, considering the wonderful smells coming from the kitchen were almost too much to bear. With dinner eaten, she walked over to the desk and keyed in her access to check the station's systems. She flipped through five pages of data and everything showed green. Not that she expected anything else. The technicians had only just left, and they would have double-checked everything before they did. She thought about going through the rest, but she yawned and her eyes burned. She would check the rest later. And if there was a problem, she was sure the automated systems would bring it to her attention anyway.

She straightened and headed towards the bedroom and her sleep suit. But when she pulled it from the case on the bed, she frowned, picked up the case, and placed both into the closet instead. Melanie slid the closet door closed, and pulling the data core from her pocket, she plugged it into the small slot in the fabricator console mounted in the wall next to the closet. The screen lit up, showing the different clothing templates she could select.

Melanie shuddered, flicking through several versions of sleep-suits. She certainly didn't want another one of those plain itchy sleep-suits. After several more flicks, she smiled. It would cost the station material from its stores, and Sofia would certainly charge her later, but right now she didn't care. She tapped 'Accept', and the wall hummed with power as it took raw materials and began to fashion them into a new item of clothing. She turned to leave, heading back to check the rest of the station's systems while the fabricator worked, when she heard a beep.

She turned back in time to see the front of the fabricator open, a chute extend with a stop, and a silky purple garment slide out. Melanie blinked. She couldn't believe it had finished so fast. The design must have had been a simpler construct than she first thought. With a big smile, she walked over to the wall and picked up the gossamer garment from the chute by its small straps, holding it up. The fabricator's chute retracted and then asked if she wanted anything else. Still in somewhat of a trance at its speed, she shook her head, tapped 'No' with her left hand, and pulled the data core from its slot, shutting down the fabricator.

Melanie smiled as she placed the silken form on the bed, kicked off her flats, slipped out of her blouse, skirt, and bra.

She picked up the purple lace and satin night dress, stepped into it, and felt the smooth caress of the fabric as she slid the straps up around her shoulders. It fit her perfectly, far better than any sleep-suit. It enhanced and drew attention to every curve instead of hiding them, and stopped only a few inches down her legs. She loved the smooth caress and the way it supported her breasts ever so gently. Stepping back to check herself in the mirror, she pulled out from a slot in the wall. She couldn't imagine why she hadn't done this long ago.

She hit the button to retract the mirror, then tapped the light control next to the bedroom door. The illumination diminished to the lowest of levels, but still let her see the outline of the bed. She pulled back the sheets, slipped between them, enjoying the feel of the soft sheets and the caress of the purple form fitting garment. Melanie smiled again as her eyelids drooped and she fell asleep a moment later.

* * *

Roy Steenson sat in the control chair of his ship the *Arthas*. The gel of the chair conformed around him, even in his battle armor, to compensate for any excessive g-forces should quick maneuvers be necessary. While the *Arthas* was only a transport, it had teeth. Cannons dotted the hull, with larger ones at the corners. And she had full stealth capability. The *Arthas* was designed to get troops behind enemy lines and attack before they could respond. At least in theory. The ship had never been used that way. Although he had used it on several stealth missions.

Roy ran another low-power scan. One of the Pinatron ships he had been following broke off of the main group, heading in a different direction. His orders were to 'stick to them like welding glue' and find out their main target. So far, nothing. He was starting to wonder if they *had* a main target in mind.

Why are these Pinatrons leaving the main group? They don't usually separate like this. While Admiral Gilbert himself told me to stick with them, he did say if there was a good reason, I could break off. After a second of indecision, Roy hit the thrusters and changed course. He tried another scan, and still couldn't see why they had separated from the larger formation. But then again, he didn't dare run the scan at full power, as the Pinatrons might detect that.

After several agonizing minutes, he tried another scan, and this time a blip appeared. Ten minutes after that, he could get enough data to tell it was one of the LV stations. And more importantly, the Pinatrons fired their engines at full thrust towards the station. *This is not good. The station should be responding by now. I'm sure they don't show up as friendly, and they must see them.*

Roy watched as the Pinatrons extended a breaching tube and attached to the main spire of the station. Roy executed a full burn towards a docking port further up the station. He thought about transmitting his SpaceGov ID, but decided against it as the Pinatrons might detect that. And the station's defenses seemed to be off. *If they can do it, so can I.*

He maneuvered towards one of the emergency airlocks several levels above where the Pinatrons had breached, hit the port thrusters to spin around and back in towards the airlock. When his ship got within five meters, the airlock's lights came on and four round metal guides extended out. The cupped ends touched Roy's ship, locked on, and gently pulled the *Arthas* towards the airlock. A few seconds later, the ship had achieved hard-dock.

He hopped out of the control couch, put on his battle helmet, grabbed his EMG353, and turned around in time to see all the lights turn green on the status panel to the right of the hatch. But when he keyed the airlock to open, it refused, asking for an authorization code. *Well, at least not all the station's security is off.* Roy punched in his Space Marine override code and his ship's exterior door slid open, followed by the station's exterior airlock door.

Roy stepped through the hatch and door, closed the outer airlock door, and turned around to face the inner door. He punched in his code again, and the door began to slide open.

Roy raised his EMG353, and dove through the door before it had opened fully. He spun, rolled, and popped up with his EMG353 pointed down the empty corridor. His helmet split along the jawline, and the upper section flipped up. The air had a fresh scent, indicating this station hadn't been operational long, but the environmental systems seemed normal otherwise. He flipped the visor back down and initiated a quick, low power motion scan. The Pinatrons were three levels below, moving slowly section by section. Pinatrons usually storm in and attempt to overwhelm a station. Not progress section by section at a snail's pace. He wondered what they were up to.

Roy brought up the schematics in his helmet's display of a standard LW station. Crew quarters should be on the next level up, followed by several levels that could be lab space. He took off down the hall towards a lift tube, his stealth boots making muted thumping sounds on the deck plates. When he reached the tube, he noticed the time above the tube's console. He winced, realizing it was the middle of the night here, and they were all likely sleeping. He hit the call for the tube and entered a few seconds later when the door slid aside.

He stepped within, hit the button for the level above, and hoped they didn't change the design on this station. The tube rocketed up, and he lept out as soon as the door opened. He ran down the corridor where the blue prints said the station manager's quarters should be.

He tapped 'Open' on the door control panel, but a 'Locked' indicator flashed. *Great, figures.* He placed his hand over the lit up locked indicator, letting the little control interface in his palm link and initiate his override. The door panel flashed an access granted, and the door split down the middle, sliding back into the wall.

Roy saw a raised shape on the bed, and he inched closer. The subdued lighting was enough to see the blanket raised in two clear areas on the upper abdomen. He went around the other side of the bed and carefully placed his hand over the woman's mouth. Her eyes shot open as she tried to scream, but all that came out were muffled gasps.

"Shhh, I'm Space Marine Colonel Steenson. I'm here to help you."

* * *

Melanie blinked at the dark shape, holding her mouth shut. He said he was a Space Marine, but she couldn't tell in the dim light. Thoughts raced through her head. How did he get aboard? The systems should have warned her. It didn't make any sense. She didn't have any weapon she could grab, not even the case she had brought from *Gemini*. It was across the room in the closet, and even if it was still next to the bed, she couldn't lift it and hit him with it before he could use that big weapon he held. At least she assumed it was a weapon from the way he gripped it.

She blinked again and realized even then it wouldn't have worked. He had a helmet on. Not knowing what else to do, she simply nodded, and the form moved the hand back from her mouth. She heard a sound of something opening. He moved away and hit the panel on the wall near the bedroom entrance. Lights dialed up to full, and Melanie squinted at the sudden change. "Who ... who are you?"

"I told you, I'm Colonel Steenson and I'm here to help you."

Melanie sat up a little, keeping the sheet pulled tightly up against her body. "Help me? I don't understand. How did you get aboard?"

Roy moved closer. "Look, there's no time for this. Pinatrons are on the lower decks, but I'm sure they will move up here soon. We need to get to the *Arthas*."

Melanie fought hard not to hop out of the bed that second at the word *Pinatrons*. "What? That's not possible! The station's systems would have told me."

"Yeah, well, they didn't tell you when I came aboard either, did they?"

"Well, no."

Roy leaned forward. "Now you see my point."

"How did you know I was here?"

Roy's helmet snapped down as he ran another low-level scan. The Pinatrons were still on the lower decks. He had never seen them move with such careful planning before. His helmet flipped back up. "This is the station manager's quarters. Where else would the station manager be this time of night? I wanted to alert you and have your assistance to help me get everyone aboard my ship."

"But I'm not the station manager."

Roy sighed and fought hard not to grit his teeth. "Look, I don't care who you are. You are in the station manager's quarters and obviously have control of this place. We need to get moving, *now.*"

Melanie pulled the sheet and blanket tighter up around herself. "Let me get changed first."

Roy shook his head as his helmet snapped shut and started another scan. "We don't have time. And besides, those standard sleep-suits are fine. Just get out of that bed!" Roy pulled the blanket and sheet away to reveal Melanie in a purple satin and lace concoction that hugged her torso and framed every curve. His eyes went wide, and he took a step back. For once, he was glad his helmet was shut. "Where in the world did you get that out here?" His altered voice came through the speaker mounted on the front of the helmet.

"Never mind! Just let me put something on!" Melanie said, jumping up out of the bed. But then pulled the sheet up around herself when she realized even though couldn't see his eyes, she could feel them run up her every curve.

Inside Roy's helmet, a pinpoint indicator turned red. "No time! We have to go, *now!*" He grabbed Melanie's wrist and yanked. The sudden action surprised her, and she dropped the sheet as her mind went numb. Before she knew it, they were outside her quarters, heading down the side corridor that linked to the rest of the quarters on this deck.

* * *

Roy stopped and held a finger up near his helmet before inching himself down towards the floor. He moved closer towards the sharp right turn where the corridor linked with the rest, reached into a compartment on the side of armor, and pulled out a long cord. Melanie blinked, wondering if he was going to tie her up. A second later, she realized it was a long snake camera. Roy fed it around the edge of the corner and an image appeared inside his helmet, showing his worst fears.

A Pinatron had stepped off of the lift tube and was heading in their direction! Even worse, he had removed the helmet to his bio-armor revealing the smooth head, pointed ears, laser sharp teeth, and flicking serpentine tongue. Roy's eyes went wide. This was something he had never seen, let alone heard of. They never removed their bio armor. The Pinatron turned towards the opposite direction, took two steps, then stopped, its faint nostril slits flared as it turned back toe talons tapping the deck plates .

Hissssss .

Roy would have swore if he could. The Pinatron must have smelled them.

Melanie shook, and Roy turned, placing his left hand on hers. It calmed her a bit, and he felt her shaking diminish. He wanted to crack his helmet and tell her it would be all right, and he could get her out of there. But he didn't dare. While the sound of the helmet's articulation was slight, the Pinatron was close enough now it might detect the sound, and that was the last thing he wanted.

Roy squeezed her hand again and Melanie looked up, her eyes focusing on the dark helmet, hoping to catch another glimpse of the soft eyes within she saw earlier. She started shaking again, and he squeezed harder, then lifted an outstretched finger towards his helmet.

She nodded in understanding and attempted to steady her nerves by wrapping her arms around herself. It didn't help, but she forced the lump in her throat down anyway.

Roy watched the Pinatron come closer, and he blew out a breath. While he was certain he could pop around the corner and fire a round from his EMG into the reptilian's head without an issue, it would bring every Pinatron up here the instant his bio-armor detected the weapons fire. He knew of only one thing to do. He reactivated the safety and sat his EMG noiselessly on the polished deck next to Melanie. Her eyes went wider than he thought possible, obviously thinking he had gone insane.

The Pinatron continued closing increasing speed and Roy slid up the wall and waited. It was only four steps away when Roy pulled a long metal serrated blade from a sheath on his right leg. A second later, he whipped around the corner. The Pinatron's eyes went wide, but that is all he managed to do as the blade dove into his neck, severing the connection to the bio-armor and killing him in the same instant. The Pinatron began to crumple as Roy grabbed him and started pulling him back towards Melanie's quarters.

Melanie saw the blade sticking out of the Pinatron's neck, and she stifled a scream as Roy dragged the body in front of her and back towards her quarters. She watched for several seconds before he stopped, that dark helmet looking at her. "Are you going to open the door or not? I kinda have my hands full here," came from the speaker on the front of his helmet. She shook her head to trying to clear the shock. Two seconds later, the spell broken, she nodded and hit the control panel to the right of the door. It split open, and Roy dragged the lifeless Pinatron inside.

Melanie looked back towards Roy's EMG . She didn't like guns, but grabbed the heavy weapon, stepped inside, and sealed the door behind her. She shuddered again, this time from the breeze from door's quick motion. "Did you have to do that? And bring him in *here?*" She sat the EMG on her desk.

Roy's helmet split and the upper half flipped up. "What

did you want me to do? Introduce us and politely ask him to leave?" Roy poked around the neck several times before removing his knife.

Melanie glared at him as she wrinkled her nose at the smell of death. "What in the world are you doing? I think he's dead."

Roy looked up. "I know that, but I want to make sure the connection to his bio-armor is completely severed, or we are going to be hip-deep in Pinatrons before we can turn around." Green blood dripped from the blade, and he wiped it on Pinatron's bio-armor before sliding it back into the sheath on his leg.

Melanie shook. "How many are aboard?"

Roy poked several more locations on the Pinatron's bio-armor. Melanie wondered what good that would do. "I'm not sure, it is hard to tell without a high-intensity scan. I do know they are all on the lower levels, except for this one. He must have come up here first. I'm sure the rest aren't far behind. Once I make sure he isn't transmitting, we have to get my ship before the rest come looking for this one." His helmet flipped shut, and he ran as powerful of a scan as he dared.

Melanie slipped off towards the bedroom and returned a minute later wearing a blouse, black pants, and matching ballet flats. Roy looked up and his helmet flipped open, revealing his jaw dangling about an inch.

Melanie smiled. "I told you it would only take me a second to change!"

Roy swallowed. "You are a lot faster than any women I have known." He looked down at her shoes. They were very feminine, matched her outfit well, and at least weren't heels. But he was sure they would make a lot of noise. "Do you have anything else? Something a bit more athletic, with a rubber sole perhaps?"

"No, I don't. And I'm sure we don't have time for me to have the fabricator make something."

"No, we don't. I checked and they are still in the lower levels. I can't tell, for certain, but they must be looking for something. Any idea what that might be?"

Melanie shrugged. "I have no idea. I just got here. The rest of the team isn't due for a couple of weeks." Her eyes went wide. "The Klarni Core!"

Roy leaned forward and stepped over the dead Pinatron . "The what?"

"We are researching a new method to extract all the energy from Klarni crystals and faster than ever before. It will give our ship's additional speed and further range. But we have run into problems, which is why we were coming out to this station."

Roy sighed. "I can imagine the Pinatrons would be very interested in such a development. But it doesn't work?"

"Not really. We have lost three ships so far. Still not sure what happened. But I do have the prototype Klarni Core here." Melanie paused for a minute and folded her arms, looking off towards the door. "But I can't imagine how the Pinatrons would have found out about it, let alone that I would be here with it."

"That's easy. You have a leak. Someone must have tipped them off. I was operating in full stealth and following a Pinatron group when one ship broke off and headed this way. I thought it was odd, so I followed. And it is a good thing I did." His helmet flipped back down. "They are moving again and heading towards my ship." His helmet flipped back up.

"If we don't go now, we won't get out of here without a firefight."

Melanie took a step forward. "We can't leave the Klarni Core for the Pinatrons ! It's only a couple of decks above us. They aren't up there, right?"

Roy glared. "No, they aren't. But if we get it, I doubt we will get back down to my ship before they reach that deck and cut us off from it. You said it doesn't work anyway. Who cares if they kill themselves off trying to use it?"

Melanie shot forward and stuck her finger in his face. "We can't let them have it! I'm sure we are close to a breakthrough!"

Roy straightened and pulled Melanie's finger from the edges of his helmet. "How sure are you of that? I doubt they could figure out what you have done and bypass problems unless they had some kind of schematics and detailed research notes." Melanie's face scrunched up as she looked off in another direction. "Let me guess, all the data on its design is with the prototype?"

Melanie turned back as her eyes drifted down. "Yes, the case has all the recent data cores."

Roy's head jutted forward as he forced all the air from his lungs in a quick fashion. "Who's brilliant idea was that?"

Melanie stood, balled her hands into fists, and put them on her hips. "Well, we didn't know Pinatrons were going to show up! And I was going to work on it until the rest of the team got here."

"Look, can you blow the station while we run for my ship?"

Melanie's eyes went wide as she leaned forward. "Blow the whole station? Seriously?"

"If it keeps technology out of the hands of Pinatrons, they could use against us, yes. Can you do it?"

"I don't know. They didn't exactly give me an owner's manual to the place. But I suppose I can try." She sat down at the desk, placed her palm on the scanning plate by the terminal, and keyed in extra access codes as they were asked. After a minute, she pointed to the screen. "I can turn off the cooling to the central reactor, it will overheat and go critical in about fifteen minutes."

"Good, do it."

"But–"

Roy leaned closer. "Look, you said yourself we can't let them have the prototype. This way they won't and we can get away. It's a win-win."

Melanie's eyes narrowed. "But all my work goes up in smoke!"

"But you will be alive to continue it. You might not be otherwise. And the Pinatrons might get it."

Melanie let out a long sigh before she brought up the station's central reactor screen. After bypassing several safety protocols, the temperature in the reactor began to rise. "There, it's done."

Roy grabbed her hand as his helmet snapped shut, and he picked up the EMG from her desk with his other hand. "Good, now let's get out of here." Melanie opened the door to her quarters, and they ran down the corridor, the quarter inch heel of her flats making slight thumping sounds across the floor. Roy winced, but they were less than what he was expecting.

When they reached the lift tube, Melanie reached forward to hit the call control when he grabbed her hand. Inside his helmet, several dots on the display had reached the upper levels. He winced as his helmet cracked open. "We can't get to the *Arthas* now. The Pinatrons have reached the level it's on. At least not get to it inside of fifteen minutes."

Melanie turned towards Roy's sealed face. "Now, what are we going to do?"

"I don't know. Can you stop the reactor?"

Melanie shook her head. "No, I can only slow it down. It was one of several safeties I had to bypass."

"Great."

* * *

Melanie stood there rubbing her forehead, trying to remember back earlier when she was in the station's configuration system. There was something digging at the back of her mind. Something she noticed, but then glossed over it. Her eyes closed as she tried to think, then snapped open. "Can you remote pilot that ship to another docking port?"

Roy leaned up against the tube door. "I suppose, but that will not help. All the docking ports are below us."

Melanie grinned. "No, they aren't. There is one emergency one off of the main lab. I noticed it in the station's systems when I was looking for something else earlier."

Roy tipped his head to one side. "That wasn't in the plans I had, and I didn't notice it when I docked."

"I don't know, maybe they put in last minute? Either way, who cares. If you bring the ship up there, we can get out of here." Melanie hit the control to call the tube towards them.

"Okay, let's give it a shot," Roy said as the doors parted and they hopped into the tube. A few seconds later, they arrived at the main lab deck, and she led him over to the massive doors. He let out a high-pitched, two-tone whistle. "Now those are some serious doors. What are you keeping in there? King Kong ?"

Melanie giggled as she leaned forward and placed her hand on the extended black panel next to the doors. It lit up, scanned her palm, and she entered several more access codes before the bolts around the door could be heard sliding back with a solid clank. "Yes, they are. And no, we don't have a giant monkey." The doors parted to their Z shape, and she pointed to the closest terminal. "There, I have unlocked everything here, it should respond to you. Get that ship and dock it above."

Roy's helmet snapped shut as he ran another scan. "And where is that, exactly?"

Her hand drifted over to point towards a tube half-way down the lab along the right wall, then shot up towards the ceiling. "That tube should go up to the airlock above. Shouldn't be too hard to find. You do know what an airlock docking port looks like, right?"

Roy's eyes narrowed inside his helmet and was glad she couldn't see his face. "Of course I do," came from the speaker on the front, "I couldn't be here otherwise."

Melanie gave him a sideways glance. "If you say so, I'm going to get the Klarni Core. You just get that ship. If you have trouble, I bet I could do it. I don't really want to be here when this place blows."

Ray cleared his throat. "I think I can handle it, Miss."

Melanie bristled at the word. "Don't give me that. I bet I can pilot it just as good as you can."

"I doubt it," Ray said with a grunt, but she had already left the lab and didn't hear.

Down the corridor, Melanie placed her palm on the control panel for the closest storage room. The scanning light came on and after a secondary scan and confirmation, the doors parted. She smiled. The Klarni Core was just as she left it. As she reached for it, all the lights above began to flash and multiple red domes –several inches in diameter– extended out along the inner walls of the coordinator and started to spin. A mechanized voice began pouring out of every speaker on the station. *"Danger.* Coolant system has failed in the main reactor. System approaching critical. All personal must evacuate immediately!" Melanie picked up the Klarni Core and ran down the corridor to the lab. She found Roy working at the terminal and swearing.

"We have to go!"

"Tell me something I don't know! This is not as easy as it looks! And those alarms are going to tip off the Pinatrons something is wrong. Why didn't you turn them off?"

"I thought I did! I told you they didn't give me the owner's manual to the place."

"Great." Roy had managed to undock the *Arthas* from the lower level and activated the thrusters on the ship, sending it straight up to the airlock above them. Roy blew out a breath as the guide rods detected the ship and extended. He hit the reverse thrusters to stop the current motion and back towards the airlock. He wanted to increase the speed, but not knowing the full torque the guide rods could take, he didn't dare.

All around them, the lights flashed faster as the voice from before boomed with more urgency. "Main reactor temperature beyond critical levels, all personal must evacuate."

Melanie rolled her eyes. "We know, we know." She looked at Roy. "How much longer?"

They heard a muted clunk coming from the tube leading up towards the airlock as the *Arthas* nestled into the guide system and pulled in, making a hard connection. Above, the airlock cycled and the inner door opened. "About that long."

They ran for the tube, climbed up the rungs into the airlock and Melanie hit her left palm on the control panel to seal it as soon as they were through. A second later, the outer door opened and Roy entered his Space Marine ID at the *Arthas* ' door. The system recognized the code, and the door slid aside. "In!"

"You don't have to tell me twice!" she said as they both ran inside. Roy slapped a control with his gloved hand, starting the door closing half a second later.

"Strap in. This is going to get rough," Roy said as he ran to the cockpit, hopped into the control couch, and began emergency procedures. Melanie had just reached one of the seats along the wall and strapped the case in her right hand in to the seat. She was about to do the same for herself when the *Arthas* executed an emergency undocking, blasting away from the airlock before it could cycle normally. The sudden change in pressure jolted the *Arthas* pushing them away from the station and sending Melanie tumbling across the decking. In the cockpit, Roy heard her fall. "I told you to strap in. You okay?"

Melanie stood up and shook her head. "Yeah, I think so."

"Well, get strapped in! That place is going to blow any second, and I hope we will be out of range."

Her eyes went wide as she dove for a seat and pulled the large thick black straps over her shoulders and locked them to the buckle extending up between her legs. "You hope?"

"I hope! It all depends on when it blows, it might–"

There was a large flash of light that reached out from behind the *Arthas* and inside every window, filling the entire ship with white light. While the glass darkened at almost the same instant, it was still enough for them to see spots for several seconds.

* * *

Melanie fought to clear her vision. The spots before her eyes finally diminished, and she unbuckled from her seat, stood up, and moved to the cockpit. Roy continued checking the Arthas' functions, but the blast didn't seem to have affected her any. Melanie looked out at the diminishing light that was LW-32 station.

As the last of the light flickered away, she looked back towards the compartment she came from and the case still buckled into the seat. She turned her head back towards Roy. "I don't suppose you are heading towards *Gemini*?"

Roy looked up. "No, I wasn't planning on it. But it is within my range, however, it will take us weeks to get there."

Melanie gave a sheepish grin, for the first time realizing she didn't care to finish the project. Her grin grew. "That doesn't matter. I'm sure we can find something to do."

Lisa

Karl squinted in the scorching sunlight. It had been months since the last rainfall and the ground stood cracked dryer than mummy dust. Standing in his khaki pants, long sleeve white shirt, and wide brim hat, something caught his eye. In the distance he could have sworn he saw a flash. His eyes narrowed further as he turned his head to the left.

There it was again.

Some sort of flash near the ground. Karl wiped the sweat from his brow and walked towards the strange flashes, passing a rock outcropping half the size of his house. Whatever it was, continued to flash, beckoning him ever closer.

Karl stood, cocking his head. At his feet lay a pair of scissors. And they looked like any normal pair of heavy plastic handled scissors, except for their odd green handle color. What was even more strange, the green spilled out onto the blades themselves? They didn't look like normal metal, yet glinted in the strong desert sun as if they were.

Karl looked around again, but saw no one. And judging by the lack of tracks, nothing had been in the area for some time. Yet, these scissors couldn't have been here long. He had come this way three days ago. His one eye scrunched up. *Could I have been that oblivious? Sure Becky had just dumped me, but to miss something flashing in my eyes like this as I walked?* He shook his head in disbelief.

He looked down at the metal instrument by his feet and it flashed at him again. Karl's eyes went wide. He wasn't moving. The angle of the sun should have remained fixed, yet he saw a flash. Something tugged at his mind to pick them up. He reached down and stopped an inch from touching the handle. What if the owner came for them? He stood back up, turned, and started walking back towards his house.

Several vultures flew above, then as if to say he passed some kind of test, glided off in a different direction.

But what if the owner returns to find a rusted pair of junk? Will they blame me? This and other thoughts whirled around in his mind and before he knew it, the scissors were in his hand.

They felt much heavier than he expected. He flipped them over in his hand, hoping for a name on the other side. No such luck. The back was as nondescript as the front.

"About time. I started to think you would never come."

Karl's head popped up and swiveled along the horizon. He saw rocks, several large saguaro cacti, and of course, scrub brush. But he didn't see anyone. "The heat must be getting to me," he mumbled.

"No, down here."

Karl's gaze zipped towards the ground, then he looked up and spun around three times, looking into the distance. But he still couldn't see anyone. He shrugged and began walking back towards his house.

"No, you dolt. In your hand."

Karl raised the scissors –that had fallen to his side– and looked closely at them. Nothing had changed. It was still the same pair of strange metal blades with a greenish handle. "I'm really losing it."

"Good grief, are all the species on your planet this dense?"

"Okay, whoever you are. The jig is up. Come, show yourself!" Karl shouted as his eyes darted back and forth across the expanse of desert rock and scrub.

Karl heard a very audible sigh. "Look, I need your help, and I am in your hand. How more specific do I need to be?"

Karl raised the scissors up again. He cocked his head. "Hello?"

"Oh, thank God! He's not a total idiot!"

"No, I am just a man that has spent too much time in the sun and is talking to a pair of scissors." He started to put them back down on the ground with the full intent of running home and never telling anyone.

"Wait! I told you I need your help! Please!"

"Yeah, right, a delusion needs my help. Uh-huh." He tried to drop the scissors the remaining inch to the ground, but they seemed stuck to his hand. "What in the world?" He stood up and pulled at them, but the plastic had adhered to his hand even though it didn't feel any different from before.

"I told you I need your help. Please!"

Karl pulled at the scissors several times, but they wouldn't budge. He would kill whoever set up this practical joke. He considered his options, but it looked like he wasn't getting rid of these things unless he played along. "All right. I will help. Now, will you please detach yourself from my hand?"

"I don't believe you."

Karl glared at the object in his hand. "Okay! Fine! I was going to throw you as hard as I could and run in the opposite direction!"

"I guess I will have to prove myself to you."

Karl rolled his eyes. "Yeah, right."

A concentrated light beam erupted from the pivot point of the blades and curved over to strike the ground in front of him. The beam shimmered, grew, then reformed, taking a humanoid shape. A head developed first, a torso followed that ended in wide hips. Slender legs and arms resolved, as did other feminine features. He watched as the head grew a face of a beautiful woman with long blonde hair. She stood naked for a second, but in an eye blink, a shimmering white gown with a deep scoop top and a skirt that ended just above her knees appeared. The material was unlike anything he had seen before. It flowed around her body like a wisp of wind.

She smiled.

"I am the Logical Independent System Array, but you may call me Lisa."

Karl stood there for several seconds open-mouthed and only noticed when a dry breeze swept past, robbing his mouth of moisture. It took him several more seconds to get the rest of his body to respond enough to make a sound. "Who ... what ... are you?"

"I told you."

"Well, you told me your name, but that doesn't tell me what you are."

"Yes, it does."

Karl shook his head. "No, it doesn't. Let's try this again. Where are you from?"

Lisa sighed. "I told you that, too. But apparently your species is even more lacking than I first feared. My Master and came here several of your days ago. However, he had to leave."

Karl smiled. *I'm dreaming. But what the heck, this is better than any of the others. Especially that one where I am in front of my graduating class wearing nothing but–"*

Lisa's hands went to her hips and a high-heeled foot began a rhythmic tapping. "Look, are you going to help me or not?"

If this Lisa was an alien, she certainly had the look of being a beautiful woman in distress down pat. "Maybe."

Lisa glared. "What does *that* mean?"

"It means I don't know who you are or how I can help you."

"But I told–"

"I need more. You said you wanted me to believe you. Well, convince me."

Lisa folded her arms over her ample bosom, which did nothing to hide them. "I thought appearing in front of you would have been all the proof you need. Considering it is far beyond your level of technology."

"Unless I am dreaming."

It was her turn to be open-mouthed. "You think I am a dream?"

"Well, to be honest, yes. I mean, I couldn't ever hope to have a girl like you interested in a guy like me. I'm just average, and you are a supermodel. And I mean, really, a supermodel that pops out of a pair of scissors? I just know the guys in white coats will show up any second."

Lisa cocked her head. "Guys in white coats? I am not sure I understand." Her body flashed, started to dissolve, then reformed. "Dang it! I cannot do this anymore. My reserves are depleted." Her body compressed back into a single beam. After two seconds, the beam looped over and into the pivot point of the scissors still in Karl's hand. "I'm sorry I couldn't hold my shape anymore. Now where were we? Oh yes, guys in white coats. There isn't anyone in the area except you and me."

Karl found the scissors were no longer stuck to his hand, and he eyed the ground where he found them. Then his gaze shifted to where Lisa was standing. Something left indentations in the desert soil. To be more specific, the marks from two high-heeled shoes were there. The kind of footprints that would have been left by a woman wearing pumps, just like what Lisa was wearing. Could a dream be that detailed? He started thinking about the whole situation again when his hand vibrated.

"Hello? Please? Help? My power levels are past critical!"

Oh, the heck with it. Even if it was a dream, Karl was not about to turn down a woman in distress. Wither she lived in a pair of scissors or not. "What do you need?"

"I told you … power … please."

"I have nothing that can charge up an alien device."

"I can make use of your electricity." Her voice cracked. "Please … hurry."

Karl ran home and sweat had soaked his clothes long before he reached the front door of his single-story ranch-style house with an angular roof. Dripping, he opened the thick light brown door and went inside, finding immediate relief from the heat. He silently thanked his cousin for augmenting his evaporation cooling system with a true refrigeration one. He only used it on days when the heat was extreme, like today. The old system could never keep his house reasonably cool on days like this.

Karl looked around the entryway and beyond for a second before he realized he had no idea how to help her. His eyes shot down to the scissors in his hand. "What do you want me to do?"

"I …" Another strange sound, as if her voice was coming apart. "I can … make … myself … fit."

"Fit where?" Karl watched as ends of the blades on the scissors changed into two long metal prongs that were 90 degrees different from the rest of the metal. The left one was even wider than the other, as if polarized.

Another strange screech. "Hurry ... can't ... "

Karl ran towards the nearest outlet behind an end table in the living room, yanked out two lamp cords and plugged the scissors into the upper receptacle. To his amazement, he didn't blow out every fuse in the old house. He thought for sure it would. "Lisa?"

No response.

"Lisa? Are you there?"

Still nothing.

Karl shrugged and decided to get a shower while she charged up. Either that or he would wake up from this crazy dream. At this point, he didn't care, although he had to admit this was the best dream he ever had.

Thirty minutes later, Karl came back down the central hallway with a wet head, fresh white long sleeve shirt, and loose khaki pants with cargo pockets on the side. He looked, smelled, and felt much better. The water hadn't woken him up, and he was starting to believe this wasn't a dream after all. He entered the living room adjacent to the front door where he had left Lisa.

The living room consisted of a black couch, two matching reclining chairs on either side with end tables, and a big flat panel TV mounted to the wall opposite the front door. The room could accommodate much more furniture, but Karl decided what he had met his needs. Besides, he never had anyone over to need anything more. One chair would have been enough.

Lisa still stood where he left her, sticking out of the outlet.

He crossed the diamond creek western rug covering his wood floor, and bent down, reaching behind the end table and towards the scissors.

"Wait! I'm not done yet."

Karl jerked his hand back. "Lisa? You're okay? Why wouldn't you talk to me earlier?"

"Yes, I am fine, thanks to you. And sorry about that, I had to convert the power properly, and it took all I had left."

Karl folded his arms, looking at the simple digital watch on his right arm. While most right-handed people prefer their watch on their left arm, Karl preferred it on his right. "How much longer?"

"Another fifteen of your minutes. And I suspect you will have a large expense from the energy I used. Sorry about that. I will help you with it."

Karl blinked taking a step back. "You took that much?" His head swiveled around, looking at the walls. "Why didn't my house burn down then? My wiring is not up to that kind of current."

"It was once I modified it."

Karl mouthed the words, "Mod-ifi-ed it?"

"Yes, or the wires would have melted long before I could get enough out of them. Don't worry, I can change them back if you want. But you will save a lot of energy if you leave them."

Karl cocked his head. "How?"

"They no longer have any resistance and can handle far above any device in this building can use."

Karl's mind spun, and a thought centered. "Superconductors? You made the wiring in my house superconductive?"

"Not just the building, but the connection to the generating facility. It was necessary or the loss would have been too excessive."

Karl blinked holding up a hand. "Wait a minute. You changed the lines? Aren't they going to notice?"

"Perhaps, perhaps not. They will notice the increased usage today, but it is doubtful anything more than that."

His palms began to sweat. "Great," Karl mumbled, "just what I need, another large bill." He collapsed into the recliner two steps to his left.

"I told you not to worry about it," Lisa paused for a few minutes, "There. They won't know a thing."

Karl cocked his head as one eye narrowed. "What did you do?"

"Nothing really."

"Lisa? What did you do?"

"Well, I adjusted your meter and changed the data on the central server as well. No one will know."

Sweaty palms grabbed the armrests of the chair as he jacked forward. "You did what?"

"I told you–"

Karl rolled his eyes as he sat back in the chair. "I know what you said, but altering them is supposed to be impossible with the new SMART meters."

"They picked the wrong name for them. The security is almost non-existent." Karl could almost feel the sly smile in the air. "I am sure even you could have made the changes."

Karl checked his watch, stood up, walked over, pulled the scissors from the outlet, and landed back into the recliner. He looked down at his hand. "Do you mind appearing again? I am getting tired of talking to a pair of scissors. I feel like a fool."

"If you like." As before, a white light emerged from the

pivot point, curved over and flowed onto the floor in front of him. He watched as the light began to take shape. A head appeared, and shoulders spread out. Her hips also expanded from the area that became her torso. Legs separated from the core light as did her arms. A moment later, Lisa stood in front of him wearing the same white dress as before. The light asymmetrical skirt had a handkerchief hem starting just above the knee in the front, showing her lovely legs and went down to her calves in the back.

Karl moved forward in his chair as his eyes went up and down Lisa's shape several times. "Wow. I know I saw it before, but wow."

She smiled. "You like?" She spun around fast, making her skirt fly out and swish back as it returned to her legs.

"Yes. You are one amazing hologram. But what I don't understand is how you created foot prints. I know all about holograms, you shouldn't be able to do that."

"Hologram?" Lisa cocked her head. "Oh I see your misunderstanding. I can generate my body via particle synthesis. It is as real as yours."

Karl's eyes went wide. "What? That's not possible."

"In your limited technology, that is true." She took a step closer, picked up a book that was lying on the black glass end table next to him, and dropped it into his lap. "Could a hologram do that? Or this?" She placed her hand on his and squeezed it. It felt warm. No way a hologram could do all of this.

"No, I guess not."

"Good, now that is settled. I need your help."

Karl blinked. "You got your recharge. What more do you need?"

She shifted from one high-heeled foot to the other. "My low energy level is not why I drew your attention."

"Then why?"

Lisa paused as if considering her words. "My Master came here to study your race."

"Study us? What for? You are obviously far more advanced. Why bother?"

Lisa nodded. "Your race is unlikely to survive. The pollution of the planet and other factors make such survival very improbable."

"Oh, I don't know," Karl said with a dismissive wave of his hand. "I think we have made great strides."

"While true, it may not be enough with the other factors. My Master was sent to investigate."

"Was sent? By whom?"

Lisa laced her fingers together behind her back as her weight shifted from one foot to the other. "His race, the Theron. They have been watching from a distance for quite some time, only now have they decided a closer investigation was necessary."

"I see. And where is he?"

Lisa sighed, walking over towards the TV then turned back a moment later. "They recalled him due to an emergency. He didn't tell me what it was, he didn't have time."

Karl shifted in his chair. He wondered if he should swallow this story or spit it out for the sheer insanity it sounded like. But looking at this woman standing in front of him that came out of a pair of scissors, he changed his mind and swallowed. "I see. Why would he leave you behind?"

Lisa's shoulders slumped as she sighed. "He didn't. Well, not intentionally. The recall beam grabbed him and he was gone. I was dropped during transport."

Karl's one eye narrowed. "So he dropped a pair of scissors while he was being 'beamed up'?"

Lisa cocked her head as she leaned forward. "Beamed up? Yes, I suppose you could use that phrase. I wasn't a pair of your scissors at the time."

"But why did he drop you?"

"The recall beam didn't have enough energy for us both. I had to stay behind."

Karl chewed the inside of his cheek. "I see." He sat back in the chair, then sprang forward again. "Wait a minute! What did you mean you weren't a pair of scissors at the time?"

"I do have the ability to change my physical appearance. Something similar to this body, but more complex." Her hands raised to her waist and lowered in a sweeping motion.

"What is your normal appearance, then?"

"I resemble one of your electronic devices, with several buttons and a small screen."

"But why would you become a pair of scissors? Your natural form sounds far more valuable looking."

"Lack of power. I didn't have that form at the time my Master was recalled. I only had enough energy for a simple shift. The scissors seemed like an easy way of getting attention without using extra power to do so."

Karl's brow furrowed. "But you had enough to appear to me in the desert."

"Yes, at the cost of almost destroying myself. I could have remained as you found me for months. That one display used up my reserves and then some."

"But why didn't you just call on my phone or something?"

"I–" Lisa's face went blank as her eyes went wide. "Never mind."

Karl threw his head back and laughed. "You didn't think of that?"

"No, I did. But I suspected you wouldn't believe me, even more than now."

"But I do believe you."

"Of course, now that I have shown myself in my entirety. What would you have done if I called you and asked for your help?"

"I might have listened."

It was Lisa's turn to laugh. "You full well know you would have hung up calling it a 'prank call' I think is the proper term. And if I had told you to come to where I was, you would have done the opposite."

Karl sighed, looking down at the scissors still in his right hand. "You may be right."

Lisa folded her arms across her chest. "You bet I am. I couldn't risk it."

Karl stood up. Lisa was taller than he thought, still she didn't quite meet him eye to eye. He tilted his head down a notch. "So what now?"

"I need your help to fly the ship home."

* * *

Karl blinked and leaned forward. "Fly the ship home? What ship?"

"You can't be that dense. Why, the one we came in of course."

"But you told me he was *beamed* back."

Lisa nodded. "Yes he was. But we came in a ship. If I am to get home, we need to use that ship. Not to mention we can't leave it around for the wrong person on this planet to find it."

"I suppose not. Or the thing explodes and takes half the planet with it."

Lisa flicked her wrist. "That is not possible. Well …technically it is, but only if several of the most unusual situations have to occur first. And the odds of that happening by accident are beyond calculation. Even the ship's destruct isn't that powerful."

Karl leaned back, shook his head, stood up, turned to the left, crossed the central hall into the kitchen.

Lisa followed. "What did you mean by that?"

Karl poked his head up from the open refrigerator. He blinked. "Mean by what?"

"Don't give me that look. I know enough about humans to realize you knew exactly what I meant."

Karl pulled out a stack of lunch meat, bread, and a bottle of mustard. "I just find it very unusual being the advanced intelligence that you seem to be, can't calculate odds. I think you are snow jobbing me." He dropped the cold items on the counter near the scissors where he had left them upon entering the kitchen.

Lisa cocked her head and blinked as she walked over to the counter island that separated them. "Snow jobbing? Oh, you mean leading you on or otherwise giving you false information to give me a further advantage."

Karl spread the mustard on the bread, assembled his sandwich and took a bite nodding. "That's the one."

"Well, it is not a matter that I can't. More that it would take a year to do so with my current physical limitations, and we don't have that kind of time."

Karl swallowed and took another bite. "I see. So why isn't your Master coming back?"

Lisa shrugged. "I don't know. To be honest, I thought he

would have returned by now. Something horrible must be going on for him to leave me and the ship alone for this long."

"And where is this ship?" Karl asked, swallowing the last of his sandwich.

"In a safe place."

"Where?"

"I am not going to tell you, but I will show you."

Karl leaned forward to smack his palms on the wooden countertop with enough force to make Lisa jump. "Listen, if you want my help, I need to know where to go."

Lisa looked towards the front door and sighed. "Very well. It is several of your miles south of here."

"Can you be more specific than that?"

Lisa grinned. "I could, but isn't that enough?"

Karl looked at the woman standing in front of him and realized he was in trouble. He could never say no to a beautiful woman. He tried to remind himself that she wasn't real, only some sort of advanced alien projection. But it didn't do any good. He rolled his eyes. "All right, I will help. Let me get my keys."

Lisa cocked her head as she reached out to touch his arm as he started moving past her. "Keys?"

"For my vehicle. I'm not going to walk for miles."

"But there are not any of your roads that will reach."

Karl smiled. "That's okay, it is a customized Jeep. I can go anywhere you need, well almost anywhere."

* * *

They bounced down the uneven terrain as Karl took pressure off of the accelerator. While the reinforced Jeep could take the rough treatment with ease, his backside was another story. As they approached another dip in the ground Lisa told him to turn. It was the third time, and he began to wonder if she was taking him in circles. The GPS on his dash said otherwise, so he kept quiet.

Karl glanced over again at the woman sitting next to him. The skirt of her dress threatening to blow in an awkward position due to the wind flowing though the open cab, but it remained in place. He didn't know if he should be happy or not about that. "How much farther? This is not a place we want to run out of gas."

"Not much more," Lisa said.

"You said that twenty miles ago!"

She looked at him. "I know, and it isn't. Trust me."

Karl chewed the inside of his cheek. "Lady, my trust in you is fading fast."

Lisa turned smiling. "It is not much more, I promise."

"It had better be. Or I am turning around and you can find yourself another patsy who will go anywhere with you without caring about the destination."

"But you did ask where."

"Yes I did! But you wouldn't tell me. That's the point!"

"STOP!" Lisa shouted and Karl slammed on the brakes. If it wasn't for their seat belts they might have been thrown into the dash. Although Karl wondered if inertia affected Lisa at all. By all known physics it should. But the again, by the same token she shouldn't exist either.

Karl unhooked his belt, stood up in his seat, and looked around. "What? There is nothing here. Nothing for miles and miles."

Lisa wasn't listening as she unbuckled her seat belt and slipped out of the Jeep, the folds of her dress flapping against her legs as she moved with increased speed to the right.

"Lisa? Where are you going?" Karl started to get out and follow when he remembered the scissors. He grabbed them from the compartment inside the armrest between the seats and took off after her. Lisa had stopped over a hundred meters from the Jeep. Karl was panting in the heat when he caught up to her. "Lisa?"

She turned towards him. Her face showed no sign of exertion or sweat, further proving her true nature. "Stand here. Do not move any closer."

Karl cocked his head. "Closer? Closer to what? There is nothing here."

Lisa smiled as she turned back. "There will be."

The ground in front of them began to swirl as if a giant whirlpool had developed in the dirt but Karl didn't feel any movement of air such a whirlpool should create. His jaw dropped as something began to rise from liquified dirt and sand. It was smooth and almost as large as his house. Roughly spearheaded on the one side, it shot back in multiple angles to split into two large projections in the back. Sunlight reflected off of the sides and not a speck of dirt could be seen anywhere even though the whole thing had been deep underground seconds before.

Karl stood there for several minutes after the whirlpool subsided. He managed to close his mouth before an insect flew in. "What ... how ... what is–"

"Impressive isn't it? I told you we were here."

"Impressive isn't the word. You really do have a ship."

Lisa turned. "Of course. Why would I say otherwise?"

Karl folded his arms. "Well it wouldn't be the first time a woman would have 'taken me for a ride'."

She cocked her head. "I do not understand the relevance. It is you who took me for a ride."

Karl unfolded his arms. "Well I got you here. My job is done." He held out the scissors. "Now you can take these and go."

Lisa held up her hands. "I can't."

"Why not?"

"It is a protocol of the Theron, I cannot carry my, I believe you would call it, 'hardware'."

"I see. Well if you open the door, I will place you inside and you can go home." Karl again wondered if he was having some very elaborate dream and would wake up any minute. Or someone was messing with his head.

Lisa shook her head causing her long blonde hair to wave back and forth. "No, that won't work either."

Karl's eyebrows met. "Why not?"

"Same reason, protocols."

"So, what do you expect me to do?"

Lisa smiled as she leaned close. "Come with me."

Karl took a step back. "You have got to be kidding!"

"Why? Have I not been truthful thus far?"

Karl took another step back and spun away, his eyes squinting in the bright light even through his sunglasses. "That is not the point," he said over his shoulder.

Lisa folded her arms. "Then what is? I can't get home without you. I need you. Please."

Karl turned back towards her. "Look, for one thing I still wonder if this is all one big dream. Granted, the best dream I have ever had, but a dream nonetheless."

Lisa smiled. "If I am a dream, then no harm in helping me."

"Well, that is only one aspect. If I am *not* dreaming, then the answer is a definite *no* I'm not leaving Earth. No matter how beautiful the alien."

Lisa seemed to blush. It was the first time he caught the emotion. It surprised him. "I know it is accepting a lot. But please, I can't do this without you."

"I don't care. I'm not leaving Earth."

Lisa stepped closer and placed her hand on his arm. "Where is your sense of adventure? I thought all humans had it?"

Karl chewed the inside of his cheek. "It disappears at the idea of leaving our planet. Or at least, it does for me." She took several steps closer, and he looked down at the feminine fingers wrapping around his arm.

"Please?"

"No. Look, you don't *have* to go home is that correct? I mean you won't die or anything."

"No I won't but if I am discovered–"

"I'm not going to tell."

"No, you don't understand. If I am discovered, I am instructed to dissolve."

Karl cocked his head while folding his arms across his chest while being careful of the scissors in his right hand. "What am I then? Chop liver?"

Lisa laughed. It started as a soft female giggle she tried to stifle which only increased until she could no longer hold back the tide causing it to erupt. Several minutes had passed until she could compose herself again. "Sorry, but you have to admit, it is rather funny."

"I have never heard of a computer understanding jokes."

"I told you, I am–"

"Yeah, yeah I know. It also explains why such an old joke would make you laugh so much. Or at least I assume that is the reason. Hey, you still didn't tell me, I discovered you, how are you still here?"

"The protocol allows for a certain stretch factor. I was able to be discovered by you, and reveal my true nature. But if more–"

"In other words, if scientists found out about your or our military–"

Lisa nodded. "Correct."

Past them a door in the middle of the ship slid open. Deep within, a high-pitched tone reached out at them. Lisa's eyes went wide. "Oh no, we must hurry."

"Why? What happened?"

"That is an alert from the sensor arrays, they have detected something approaching from the south. Several vehicles. I suspect the ship has attracted unwanted attention."

Karl shook his head. "That is not possible. There is no way they could have located this ship that quick."

Lisa expanded her link to the ship's systems and displayed an image in the air hovering above her hand. "Then what do you call these?"

Karl blinked at the large military vehicles heading towards them at top speed. Leading were several jet-powered aircraft. They would be here in a few minutes judging by the amount Lisa had to zoom out to give him the distance. And behind them were helicopters, and the numerous land vehicles. "I don't understand, how would they have found this so fast?"

Lisa sighed. "It is possible they detected the signals I used to navigate you here. I didn't think it was a frequency you normally monitored."

"Perhaps not, but it might have grabbed someones attention by accident." Karl pointed towards the open door, grabbed her wrist and pulled as he started moving. "Either way, get in. I'm sending you home."

Lisa blinked. "But–"

"Yes, I'm coming too. I'm not going to let you blow yourself up when I could avoid it." He stepped inside the doorway and Lisa followed.

The ship felt even bigger inside he originally thought, even though it looked large from the outside. It was very comfortable, even roomy. What surprised him was the controls on the wall looked like they were designed for human hands. "Well, I suggest we get this bucket of bolts moving. Those jets are going to be here any minute."

Lisa moved forward to the cockpit, sat in one of the chairs, and pointed to the one next to her seated in front of a large sloping console. Karl followed, placed the scissors in a side pocket on his leg, and sat in the larger chair. As soon as his body touched the material at the back of the chair, the area in front of them lit up with an overhead map displaying the incoming jets. Lisa closed her eyes and craft all around Karl rumbled, but stopped a few seconds later. "Oh no. It won't accept my command to return."

"Why not? You seem to have control of everything else here?"

"I do. But my Master left a protocol I didn't know about."

"Uh-oh. That don't sound good." Karl looked around expected to be zapped any second. "I take it my life is forfeit?"

Lisa blinked. "What? No! We wouldn't kill anyone! But the ship won't leave with you aboard."

"And you can't leave without me either."

Lisa sighed as she hung her head. "Yes." She bit her lip. "Karl, get back to your Jeep and head as far away as you can."

"And leave you here?" He shook his head. "No way, so get that thought out of your pretty head right now."

"We don't have a choice. I cannot let this ship fall into

another race's hands. Besides, if I don't do it, the ship will on its own."

"And make one large hole in the ground."

Lisa shrugged. "Yes. I hate to, but there is not any other option."

"How about that dissolving thing you could do? Why not do that to the ship?"

"It is possible, but would take too long to set up. It's not a normal Theron protocol. Please Karl, we don't have time for anything else. It was nice meeting you."

"Can you still send this thing home?"

"Yes if–"

Karl didn't wait for her answer as he stood up, he held his hand over the scissors sticking out of his side pocket, and darted towards the hatch which slide open at his approach. Lisa ran after him. "Karl! What are you doing? You have to leave me here!"

Karl didn't say anything, he only kept running. Thirty seconds later he reached the Jeep, hoped behind the wheel and gunned the engine. Dirt spit out from beneath the tires as Lisa managed to grab one of the supports and flip herself into the seat beside him. "Karl! You must stop and put me back!"

Karl turned his head. "No I don't." He pressed the accelerator down to the floor. Dust clouds obscured everything behind them. "Listen, give it another ten seconds then send the ship home. I suspect if you have it lift off at full power, the jets won't see much by the time they get here. Unless they have already found it."

Lisa smiled. "No they won't. The ship is covered in a material that prevents detection unless they are almost on top of it. They are only investigating due to my mistake."

"Unless we are still too close, launch that sucker."

Lisa nodded and behind them they heard a faint wine. Karl looked in his rear view mirror and managed to see a white shape levitating up into the sky. It started slow bit increased its speed exponentially. A few seconds later no sign remained other than the slight movement of dust on the ground. Overhead they heard two jets streak past.

Karl looked over. "I suspect we will get stopped by them. We could try to outrun the ground vehicles, but I can't hide from a jet or helicopter."

Lisa nodded. "I understand."

The Jeep lurched on the rough terrain. "I'm sorry, I couldn't send you home."

"You did your best. And I did upload a message into the ship's systems. The Theron will know what happened, and will come for me."

Karl smiled. "So all is not lost then?"

Lisa smiled back. "Not at all."

"Good, now can you put something else on?"

Lisa cocked her head looking down at the gossamer dress she wore. "Why? Don't you like it?"

"I do. Very much so. However, those we are likely to bump into will wonder why you are out in the deep desert wearing a dress and heels."

"It will take extra energy to change."

"I don't think we have a choice."

Lisa nodded. "Very well."

Out of the corner of his eye, Karl saw her outline below her neck grow more white, almost glowing, enlarge, then retract revealing a tight long sleeve shirt, tight jeans, and high-heeled leather boots that went up to her knee. "While better, that is not what I had in mind, but I guess it will have to do. I'm not going to have you waste power by changing again."

Lisa's eyebrow raised. "What do you mean?"

"That is not exactly desert wear. It is close, but a little more loose and no heels."

Lisa smiled. "I like these. And unless I am mistaken, so do you."

"Yes, but not for the right reasons," Karl muttered.

"What was that? I believe the Jeep's noise blocked me from hearing what you said."

"Nothing." Lisa's scissors threatened to jump out of the cup holder he had shoved them into when he leapt into the Jeep. His fingers grabbed the bouncing metal. He lifted them up. "Can you do something with these?"

"I can't get rid of them, you know that. They are as much a part of me as breathing, I think is the proper phrase."

Karl bounced again in his seat and he was amazed Lisa did the same thing. If he didn't know better, he would have thought a real woman sat beside him. "I don't mean that. You mentioned changing the form, could you please change them? I am tired of getting poked by your, uh, hardware."

Lisa giggled. "Very well." The scissors in his hand began to glow and when the light faded a compact cellphone sat in their place.

"Perfect!" Karl said placing the new phone in his pocket. Above he heard two jets and the thump thump thump of helicopters. In the distance he saw all-terrain land vehicles heading in their direction.

"Looks like we are going to have company." Lisa smiled as she slid the seat belt across her chest and locked it.

Karl slowed down and turned towards Lisa. "Whatever you do, act natural."

The Run

Keefe squeezed the made-to-order synth-leather encased controls as they nosed their way into the docking bay. He looked over to Eos who sat on the other side of the spacious bridge. The man leaned forward in his chair, checking the readouts from several screens.

Burch grunted as he raised his massive non-human frame from the single seat behind them. He jerked a long green thumb over his shoulder. "Well I'm gonna check the cargo. I know they will want it as soon as we dock." He lumbered his way through the circular hatch at the back wall as it opened. A second later it sealed itself behind him with a solid whoosh, followed by a clink of the lock.

Eos turned his attention back to the screen below his nose. He twitched within his blue flight suit with pent-up energy. "We are cleared for pad 5543, I just got confirmation."

Keefe snorted. "Took them long enough. We have been on approach for hours, and only now, after we have passed the bay doors, do they give us a place to go?" The automatic docking thrusters kicked in to slow their approach further. Even at the reduced speed, they felt the change in inertia.

"Hey this is a *lot* better than that time we were docking at

Doleron 3," Eros said, never looking up from his screen.

Keefe shuddered remembering, causing him to grip the controls tighter. A bead of sweat trickled down inside his matching blue flight suit with the name *Mortania* stiched into a patch covering both shoulders. His name matched the ship's in design and color, but placed over a pocket on the left side of his chest. He never thought the suits were worth the extra expense, but Eos insisted their clients would take them more seriously with a uniform look. Not to mention, be willing to pay more. Keefe's head swiveled towards Eos. "You aren't kidding. I didn't think we would make it out of there."

"We did by the skin of our plating."

Keefe laughed relaxing a little as his gaze returned to his controls. "Although that might have improved the old tub's looks, it was a real bucket of bolts. Do you remember how I often had to jiggle the controls so they would register?"

"How could I forget? You kept telling me every time we docked they were 'just like a stubborn woman, you had to know how to push the buttons'." Eros turned his attention back to the various screens surrounding him, checking their approach. Tapping several controls, he requested a verification check. With what they were hauling, it wasn't worth the risk of lost time due to botched approach. Not to mention, the station personal might take an interest if they did anything out of the ordinary.

Keef rolled his eyes then shook his head. "Well, she was! Just pulling back wouldn't make it go up. Oh no, I had to wiggle the controls back and forth while I did it. I never understood why you didn't fix that."

Eos shook his head, looking towards Keefe as his eyes narrowed. "Hey if you remember, I tried several times. I think she liked your touch."

"Nah, nothing held together on that bucket." Keefe thought of the times he had to run back to the stabilizer control to kick it before they crashed. Or that when they fixed the stabilizer, the retros failed. And if they were working, the gyro went haywire. Not to mention the whole ship stank of Trigilion wine. A previous owner must have spilled a load during the ship's long life and, try as they might, they could never get rid of the vile smell.

"Especially on that trip, nothing went right. They wouldn't give us a final clearance even though we got confirmation days before." Eos sat back in his chair, causing the new self conforming gel to generate a slight squeak. Through the window in front of them that extended the full width of the bridge, he watched the immense station turn below them as the automatic thrusters again fired locking them into matching rotation with the rest of the station. The ship slowed as it descended to pad 5543.

Keefe winced as thoughts bubbled up from the past. "Who picked Doleron 3 during the middle of the Kilrarin war? Hmm?" He tapped several controls double-checking the auto docking system was functioning properly. "I mean, really, who wants to fly in the middle of a firefight? There were energy blasts all around us the whole flight in and out."

Eos took a deep breath, thankful he didn't smell Trigilion wine. "Hey, we made it, didn't we?"

"Yeah, as you say, by the skin of our plating."

"The Doleron's *did* protect us." Eos tapped a panel to his right, making sure there were no new messages from docking control. That time on Doleron 3, their landing point kept changing every few minutes. They flew for hours inside the station until a controller had pity on them, gave clearance to land on a nearby pad, and locked out any further changes. *If the Doleron's had known what we were hauling, they would have let us dock within two minutes.*

Keefe gritted his teeth. "Some protection! Only after we were in spitting distance of their station did they do anything!"

"I knew you could out fly the Kilrarin's," Eos said, folding his arms and turning his chair towards Keefe. "You are the best pilot I have ever seen. Besides, you knew we were hauling trinium for their reactors. The Doleron's were paying a fortune with the war going on."

"Uh-huh, that is because no one was *stupid* enough to actually try going there. Heck, you never told me what jump coordinates you entered. We popped out of hyperspace in the middle of a Kilrarin battle blockade and only *then* did you tell me it was Doleron 3!"

Eos grinned. "Well, you could have spun up the jump drive and got us out of there."

Keefe snorted. "On what? Fumes?" We didn't have enough for a short jump, much less get us to another system! My genius navigator didn't take that into account. We could have topped off the tank at Elog 4, it was on the way. But ohhh noooo you had to put in the direct route without a pit stop,"Keefe grumbled.

"Well ... " Eos said, looking back to the hatch then at Keefe. "We could have."

"How?"

"I stashed a little extra fuel inside the cargo hold port side wall, just in case."

Keefe's chair turned towards Eos, his face red. "You mean we could have jumped *out* of that hellhole at any time and you didn't tell me!"

"Well …we needed the credits. It took every spare one we had for that load of trinium. Sure, we could have sold it elsewhere, but it might have been at a loss." Eos shrugged.

Keefe's eyes narrowed. "Maybe, but you should have trusted me with that info. We dogged energy cannons, mines, and drones for that delivery. With the Kilrarin's on our tail the whole way in *and* out."

"But you did it. And I always thought hiding on the back of one of their cruisers was pure genius."

"Yeah it was, until the stasis lock failed, we slid off, and the others fired double blasts at us."

Eos laughed. "It didn't hit us though. Even with the thruster control shorting at the time, you dodged every shot."

Keefe smiled as he turned back to the controls and activated the final sequence, landing them gently on the pad. "True, and I would hate to have been the captains of those cruisers. They blasted the bridge off of their own ship."

Eos smiled, stood up, took two steps, and put his hand on Keefe's shoulder. "Admit it, you miss that old bucket and dodging Kilrarin's."

Keefe sighed. "I suppose, at times, maybe. But I still love this ship far more." He patted the controls affectionately.

"Well, you know without that run we wouldn't have her."

"True. And in the end the Doleron's beat the pants off of the Kilrarin, well if they wore pants. So it all worked out." He turned his chair around and jerked a thumb towards the hatch as it irised open. Keef smiled as it opened without issue, remembering being locked in the tiny cockpit of the bucket for hours while he tried to fix the malfunctioning hatch. "Well, let's go, we have a delivery to make."

The Storm

Bud sighed as he looked at his screen. The storm was a monster, to be sure. Bigger than anyone had ever seen. Many had seen ionic storms like this in the past, but this one was a category 7 when the scale only went to 5. Outside, he could see through the bridge window the red and gold colors flashing into a chaotic mass that personified the raging torrent that existed just beyond the ship.

Looking back, he tapped the screen trying to find a safe path for the *Serburus* –his old but very reliable freighter– to skirt around. But it wasn't working. He had enough Trilium fuel to go through it, not around. And through wasn't an option. Or at least, not an option where he would live.

Iconic storms of this magnitude blasted through anything electronic, wiping it clean. Worse, it did the same for neurons. While people had survived such storms, their minds were another story.

Bud leaned back, put one large booted foot on the edge of the console, then raised his other foot to cross the first at the ankle. Two options, and neither worked. He knew he should have never taken this job. The payoff was too good. And like his father always said, if the deal is too sweet, check for poison.

Dang, why did he have to be right now of all times. Bud's synth leather jacket squeaked as he folded his hands behind his head and glared at the deck plate above. There were a few specks of rust, but otherwise the plate looked new. While the *Serburus* was an old ship, Bud had kept her in fine condition. He even upgraded the systems on several occasions.

He sniffed the air wafting from a nearby vent and sighed. The system needed more filters and a good scrubbing ...*again*. Something else that *really* needed an upgrade.

His eyes gleamed as he sat up quickly. The last engine upgrade! That was it! He could rig the new accumulator to take an alternate fuel supply. Tapping his screen, he found his cargo of Matrox-33 could do the job, but it would consume over half of it.

Too much. If he didn't deliver at least three-quarters of this cargo, the Alliance would not be happy. And when they weren't happy, someone died.

"Irma? Is there anything we can do?"

The *Serburus'* AI appeared on a nearby screen. A beautiful woman with slim features and long dark hair that cascaded down her neck smiled at him. "I wondered when you were going to ask me."

"Yeah, yeah, save me the speech of how smart you are and tell me what we can do."

"I think you know the answer to that."

He folded his arms as he leaned closer. "Humor me."

"Very well. It is possible to go through, but only the ship itself would survive. We would not. However, it is possible to go around using the Matrox-33 in addition to our current fuel."

Bud rolled his eyes. "Yes, but the Alliance wouldn't let me live very long after, either."

"True, you would live longer going through the storm."

"If you call that living. I would be a vegetable."

Irma's eyes narrowed. "And I wouldn't even be that."

"Touché, there must be something else we can do? Shield us perhaps?"

Irma shook her head, long hair flicking back and forth. "Not possible. The storm is too strong. It will penetrate the shields in a matter of minutes."

Bud rubbed his chin. "A matter of minutes, eh? How long exactly?"

Irma blinked. "Not enough."

"Irma, I didn't ask if there was enough, I said how long!"

Irma sighed. "10.3 minutes"

"And it will take us twenty to get through at full burn?"

Irma smirked. "Correction 21.7"

Bud rolled his eyes again. "Okay 21.7 Hmm, I wonder if that is enough."

"Enough for what? Either way, we will not survive."

"If I remember correctly, Matrox-33 has a unique reaction when combined with several elements. One being our fuel."

"Yes ... it explodes."

"But what if we combine them–in a very limited fashion–in the accumulator while directing the energy output?"

Irma's eyes darted around as she ran several intense calculations. "It still explodes."

"But will the new engines be able to utilize it?"

Irma's image gave a very human shrug. "I have no idea. Nothing in my data says it has been done, let alone if it could be done."

"Can you guess?"

"I cannot guess. I can only make an extensive extrapolation based on the data given to me."

"Then what is the result of your extensive analysis?" Bud grumped.

"I believe your favorite phrase 'up a creek' fits the situation."

"Great." Bud ran his hands over and down his face, then took a deep breath letting it out slow. "Any sign of the storm dissipating?"

Irma shook her head again. "Negative. While a storm of this size should not be able to maintain its structure for a per longed period, the internal density is more than we have encountered before. Dissipation might not occur for many months."

Bud's eyes flashed in thought. "Irma, why don't you think the mixing of the Matrox-33 and our fuel will work?"

"I thought I was explicit enough. We will explode."

Bud rolled his eyes. "I know that, but how exactly?"

"I don't see the point. The result is the same."

There were times like this when Bud seriously considered having the AI's personality toned down a bit. She sounded too much like his ex-wife. His eyes blazed as his teeth clenched. She did sound like her, too much in fact. He looked again at the screen and realized she also had a similar resemblance to his ex-wife. He thought back and realized the changes must have been so gradual that he didn't notice until now. She definitely wasn't like this when he had her installed. *Garon! He is going to get it when I get back to Andrais.*

Bud forced his emotions back as he looked out the window at the storm raging beyond. "Irma, humor me."

"Very well. The energy created in the accumulator will

be too much for the system to handle at approximately 10.5 seconds into the procedure."

"Why?"

Irma's eyes narrowed, showing her irritation. "I told you, we explode."

"Yes, but what exactly happens first? Does the accumulator breach? Or something else?"

"No, the raw energy backlash floods the system, overwhelming the accumulator, causing a rupture that destroys the ship."

Bud rubbed the stubble on his chin. "Then it might work."

Irma blinked and cocked her head to one side. "If your goal is our destruction, then yes, it will."

Bud sat back in his chair, folding his hands behind his head. "No, that is not my goal. But I think we may have a solution."

"How?"

"Ten seconds is quite a while when dealing with this kind of reaction, isn't it?"

Irma nodded. "I suppose it would depend on your point of view."

Bud sat back up and smiled. "That is true. But I think it is a long time. I assume the reason we explode, besides the power backlash, is because the system can't utilize it quickly enough?"

Irma nodded again. "That is correct."

"Then our solution is simple. We vent that energy build up through the shields."

Irma blinked. "But that–" her eyes darted around her screen in thought "might actually work."

Bud's grin widened. "Thank you. It should increase their protection and usage time. The question is, will it give us enough time to get through? Not to mention, will we have enough Matrox-33 to make our contract?"

"Impossible to estimate at this point."

Bud gritted his teeth. "Fat lot of help you are. You can collate a tremendous amount of data, but when it comes down to it, I would have more help with a roll of the dice!"

Irma glared. "I can only deal with data I have. This is a total unknown."

"Take a guess then."

"I do not–"

Bud sighed and gave a short grunt. "Just give me odds."

"Impossible to calculate at this time."

Bud bit the inside of his cheek. "Okay, then answer me this: Would you rather I rip out your core, stuff it in a life pod, and leave you adrift here?"

Irma's one eye scrunched up. "I am not sure."

Bud sighed again. Just like any other woman he had dealt with, they never gave a straight answer. "Great. Long odds then."

* * *

Bud's muscles rippled as he dragged the third container of Matrox-33 into the cramped engine room and connected it to the holding tank he had installed. Oval, with several connection points leading off at the top, he knew it would lower the pressure of the Matrox-33 before it was injected into the accumulator sitting next to it. And should result in an increased reaction stability.

He thought about using the anti-gravs to move the Matrox-33 but decided against it. The stuff was too touchy in the best of circumstances. Granted, he had taken every precaution and used the best shielding on the containers, but why take the risk when he could do it himself. This was one of the times his large, muscled frame came in handy. The downsides were more common as several areas of the ship were too narrow for his wide shoulders, forcing him to move sideways.

Checking the connections were secure, he opened the valves. Pure liquid Marox-33 flowed into the holding tank without incident. "There, that should do it. And everything is holding."

Irma appeared on a screen that held a diagnostic readout a second before. "For now. That tank is not rated for this usage."

Bud spun around. "Don't do that! I might have accidentally increased the flow rate."

Irma smirked. "That would have been bad."

"No kidding! I– Wait, since when do you do sarcasm?"

Irma blinked as the side of her mouth displayed a slight curl. "Whatever do you mean?"

Bud bit down hard on the inside of his cheek. *That settles it, she is getting an overhaul at the next opportunity. I'm not waiting until I see Garon.* His eyes narrowed. "Yeah right. Check the system. Everything check out?"

"I would have told you otherwise."

He double-checked the flow and lines to be sure, turned, left the engine room, and sealed the doors.

Irma popped up on a nearby screen next to the ladder. "Why did you bother locking the doors? If something goes wrong, they are not going to be of any help."

"It might buy us a few seconds."

"To do what? If the system fails, the shields will shut down, and we will die."

"You are such a bundle of optimism today," Bud said through gritted teeth.

Irma shrugged. "I am only stating the obvious." Her image disappeared.

Bud climbed the ladder up to the bridge. He sat in his chair and ran a quick check of all systems. He tapped in several commands and a bluish energy envelope snapped into being around the *Serburus*.

Irma's image appeared adjacent to Bud's main screen. "Shields are online at normal strength."

"Good. Activate the Matrox-33 infusion. I'm counting on you to adjust the flow as needed."

"I thought you said I could leave if I wanted?"

Bud smiled. "I lied. Now keep an eye on that flow."

Irma nodded as Matrox-33 began to flow into the accumulator, mixing with the fuel already there. Bud jammed down hard on the thrust controls and the engines activated, sending a golden hue out of the exhaust cells. They shot forward with enough force to shove Bud back in his chair. A second later, the Matrox-33 mix reached critical mass, causing a massive surge of energy to rush out and slam out of the accumulator.

Irma redirected the extra energy into the shields. The blue bubble around the ship increased in size and density as the golden hue radiating out from the engine exhaust cells tippled, pinning Bud into his chair with the sudden acceleration. Sparks bounced off of the bubble as ionic energy collided with them.

Bud grunted under increased gravity. "Status?"

"Speed twice normal and increasing. Shield density is blocking all ionic activity. However, I am detecting a failure in one of the emitters on the port side."

Bud tried to reach for the controls but couldn't move. G-forces had him pinned. "How ... how bad?"

"In normal situations, I could compensate. With the storm, I cannot do so, or we will lose integrity for a microsecond. Something we cannot afford."

Bud gritted his teeth harder as the g-forces increased. "Yes, keep them up or we will fry. Any chance it will hold?"

"Unknown." A monitor flashed red, with one line displaying several numbers. "Emitter three is nearing critical. Total failure in one minute."

Bud's knuckles turned white as he gripped the chair that held him pinned. "How ... how long until we are clear of the storm?"

"Five minutes at current speed."

"Increase the flow."

"But I do not know if I can maintain stability."

"It is either that or we end up with a brain wipe."

Irma nodded. "Acknowledged. Flow increased, speed also increasing."

Bud felt as though ten of the Matrox-33 cylinders were sitting on his chest. "No shit Sherlock!"

Another monitor flashed red. "Emitter failure imminent. The extra energy is causing added stress."

"Blow it out the communications dish," Bud wheezed.

"But that will fry the whole system."

"We don't have an option. Do it!"

Irma nodded and a massive wave of raw energy flashed up from the base of the dish that sat on top of the *Serburus'* hull as energy bolts flickered along its edge. The bolts grew in intensity before arcing towards the center like giant spider legs. They collided with each other, combining, before erupting out of the cone shaped dish a second later at the center focus point in a massive wave of yellow-blue energy that lashed out into the storm. The wave coalesced the ions, carving a large swath through the otherwise chaotic nightmare.

Bud looked out the window, seeing the stars clearly through an otherwise red and gold haze. "Go through that! The shields should hold!"

Irma nodded and changed the *Serburus'* course. Bud grunted and he bit down hard. "Not so fast, I can't–" The words were cut off as he blacked out from the increased gravity.

Bud opened his eyes and sat up. The acceleration that held him in place was gone. Irma's face appeared on the large center screen. "Well, lookie who is finally awake!"

Bud rubbed his head. "Irma, I'm not up for more of your sarcasm. How long have I been out?"

"Two hours."

Bud jumped to his feet, then fell back into the chair when they felt like rubber. "Two hours! Why didn't you wake me?"

"I tried, but you were out like a blown engine."

He sat back down and leaned back. "Status? I assume we got through."

Irma nodded. "I would think that is obvious, considering we wouldn't be speaking otherwise. And before you ask, yes we are back on our original course. The added boost should have us arriving later tomorrow."

Bud's eyes went wide. They were over five days out before entering the storm. "That much? What's our speed?"

"While I have managed to decelerate us quite a bit using a nearby gravity created by the storm, we are still at 3.5 times normal speed."

"That could be a problem when we arrive. Without

communications, we won't be able to tell them we need help in slowing down."

"Negative, I can use the planet's atmosphere as a breaking system."

Bud glared at her. "How? Aren't the shields offline?"

"Not since I have bypassed the failed emitter. They will hold long enough if I use a slow braking maneuver."

"Are you sure?"

Irma's eyes narrowed. "You doubt me now? After I got us through?"

Bud held up his hands. "Okay, you're sure." He turned and started heading down the ladder to the lower decks.

A screen flashed on next to the ladder with Irma's face. "Where are you going?"

"To check on the Matrox-33. If we don't have enough, we might need to change course."

"How? We don't have enough fuel to do that."

Bud sighed. "Point taken."

Down in the engine room, he unhooked the Matrox-33 cylinders from the holding tank, dragged them back to the cargo bay, and locked them in place with the others. One was empty, but the other two still had over half capacity. He did a rough calculation in his head, and it should be enough. But it was going to be close. He hoped the Alliance representative was in a good mood when he arrived. Or they didn't add extra taxes.

Bud shrugged. No sense in worrying about it now. Nothing he could do about it. He checked over the rest of the ship and made his way to his cabin. He tapped the screen near his cot. "Irma? I'm going to rest for a bit. Wake me if anything changes in our status."

"If you recall, I didn't mange to wake you last time," she said out of the corner of her mouth.

"Next time use a louder method," Bud said with a smile before he pulled off his boots, climbed into his cot, and closed his eyes.

Several hours later he awoke to blaring marching band music that banged around inside his head long after it stopped being broadcast over the speakers near his cot. "Irma! I am awake! What is it?"

"Nothing. I was just testing the system to make sure I could wake you."

"You what!"

"Well, I needed to know. Method is verified. You can go back to sleep."

"Fat chance of that!" Bud said, climbing out his cot and bumped his head while trying to stand. He still felt a little groggy. He slid his boots back on and, after several tries, managed to tighten the laces. By now the sleep had been driven from his mind, and he headed up to the bridge.

Bud sat in his chair with enough force to make the synth leather complain. "How far are we from docking?"

"We are five hours from breaking and one more for actual docking, making it six hours total."

"Great. Six hours alone, in the same room with my ex-wife."

Irma blinked. "What?"

Bud sighed as he sat back. "Never mind."

The Transport

Kiandra swore as another blast impacted the shields. They were in trouble and she knew it. Jake pulled at the helm control, adjusting their course again. "It is no good captain, I can't maneuver fast enough. The *Isanguard* is a transport, not a fighter."

"I know Jake, just do what you can. At least we are giving them a challenge." Kiandra's face cracked into a half grin.

"Wish I could be more of a challenge!" Jake yanked the controls into a free fall spin then back up so fast even the inertia dampeners couldn't eliminate the effect on their stomachs.

Kathy looked down at her console and frowned. "They are jamming us sir, I can't get a signal past them."

Kiandra's brows met. "Even the new theta frequency?"

Kathy nodded. "Yes sir, it was the first one I tried. What I don't understand is, who are they?"

"I think I have a hunch. Jego? Did you get a scan before we raised shields?"

The blue skinned Tirsaian nodded. "Yes sir, but I couldn't determine the designing species."

Kiandra gripped the command chair tightly as another blast hit the shields head on. "Any traces of element U334?"

"Why yes. Is that significant?"

"Sadly yes, it is the Sonairans."

The whole bridge crew turned to face Kiandra. "The Sonairans?" they said in unison.

"Yes, rumors high up in Earth Force said the Sonairans might have been amassing for an attack. And I think we got too close for their comfort."

"But why now, after centuries of peace?" Kathy shook her head.

"Well, officially, we never did find out why they stopped themselves last time. But I have always suspected that another threat, larger than Earth Force, needed their full attention. And now it with that situation handled, they have decided to pick up old gauntlets." Kiandra cringed as another blast raked the ship.

"Captain, shields are almost gone. We can only take another hit or two." Brett tapped several commands into his engineering console.

"We need to get away and warn Earth Force. Head for the asteroids." Kiandra pointed to the large belt of blasted rock far off to the starboard side of the *Isanguard*.

Brett's eyes wend wide. "Sir? Begging your pardon, that is suicide. With our shields so low and the damage we have already sustained–"

Kiandra glared at Jake. "I gave you an order. I am confident you can outmaneuver the hunks of rock in our path. The ones shooting at us may be another story."

"Yes sir," Jake said as he gunned what was left of the engines and pulled the controls to the right.

"Hey Kiandra? Earth to Kiandra? Are you in there?" Isaac said, waving his hand in front of her face.

"Huh? Yes, I am here." Kiandra blinked, shifting in the uncomfortable green vinyl bus seat as the tire below them hit another pothole and shook the entire bus.

"Are you sure? I was talking to you."

"I am fine," she sighed, "I just have a lot on my mind."

"Oh? I don't see how. It is only the first week of school. We haven't got into anything heavy yet."

"Just because you haven't paid attention doesn't mean that a lot has happened in the past week." Kiandra glared at the boy looking back from the seat in front of her.

"Well, sorrrry. What put the burr under your saddle?" Isaac turned around and plopped back into his seat with a small thud. Isaac thought about Kiandra. Every time he tried to talk with her, she seemed to be miles away. He knew she didn't have a boyfriend, but her beautiful long blond hair and young curves had many guys interested. However, she wasn't interested in them. While many had tried, Isaac was determined to be the one that got through.

"Captain, you were right. The asteroids are interfering with whatever they were jamming us with. The theta frequency is working again," Kathy said.

"Good, send Earth Force our coordinates and tell them to send everything they have. The Sonairan fleet has to be very close for them to risk attacking us like this." Kiandra sat back in her padded captain's chair, the only thing she liked about being in command of the *Isanguard* at this moment. "Tell them the fleet must be along our original flight path."

"But if their exposure is such a threat, why didn't they send more ships after us?" Jego checked his scanners again, making sure other ships hadn't joined in.

"I suspect they figured one ship was enough when they could keep us from contacting Earth Force. At least–" Kiandra swore in slow motion as another highly charged stream of energized ions impacted their focused energy shields. Her head turned thirty degrees as a large smooth panel, a foot to the right of her captain's chair with its high back and captain's controls mounted into the armrests, flickered. The flicker was slow, then began to increase its deadly dance of light and dark until a spark started in the corner of the panel. It grew exponentially, reaching to the center where it joined energy streams from the other corners, creating a deadly bloom of electrical energy which grew in size until the internal conduits could take no more. The blast started inside, beneath the control panel itself, then expanded outwards in a large rupture of energy that sent particles of the panel flying in multiple directions. She looked back to see the giant hole where one of the *Isanguard's* shield regulators called home. The alternate source, further down the rusted but worn smooth decking, tried to keep up, despite its reduced stature.

The *Isanguard's* edges came to life as a tightly focused beam of energy impacted the shields, sending the ship in the opposite direction on a spiraling arc through space that sent every stomach into a tailspin. Another barrage missed the main energy protection bubble, but it hit the secondary one, causing more of the reactor's greatly needed energy to evaporate.

Above Kiandra, hidden in the upper layer of the bulkhead, a tiny fissure started in the energy distribution web. It suddenly mushroomed into an all out leak, burning through insulation and joining other lines carrying power. As they joined, the level of energy burst out in a cloud of particles containing gas and insulation. The bulkhead groaned under the sudden stress, sending micro fractures throughout its mass. The cracks spread out in a destructive radius until several met, causing the large portion of the ceiling to succumb to the gravity and inertia of the latest maneuver. It fell down behind Kiandra, sending lighted, sparking conduits swinging in her direction. She quickly ducked as one of them swung in an arc that missed her head by a micron, but a spark shot out, digging into her face. The cable continued on its swing until the other end could hold no longer and the beaten and fraying composite structure ripped apart, letting the cable continue on its way until it impacted the center of a status screen on the opposite side. Another spark from the cable reached into the already damaged screen circuits and overloading them, causing it to expand outward to relieve the energy that now had nowhere else to go. Acrid smoke poured from the new fissure, wrenching any lungs that dared breathe it.

Throwing the bits of insulation, dirt, dust, and bulkhead aside, Brett tried to reach one of the alternate consoles that still glowed brightly. He tapped the normally smooth, but now pitted and etched glass panel as it attempted to read his quick movements. Another groan from the metal above as the thrust systems fired again, sending Brett flying into the metal wall in the opposite direction.

Outside, one of the thrusting beams flickered, sparked, then imploded under the unusual strain. The loss of one gave the others extra power that sent the ship in an even more erratic maneuver. Kathy's stomach could hold no longer, and she leaned away from the communications controls as hot liquid splashed onto the dirty deck plate.

Jego's blue hand wiped the dirt from the glass panel under

his nose, etching it in the process. The indicators showed the other ship's power systems flickering as energy built up in one area of the ship with exponential speed, then erupted outward in a tightly focused blast that reached out, squeezing their shields in an iron grip. The screen glowed brighter yet, wavered, then faded from existence. Jego swore in his native Tarsaian as he leapt from his console, and in a heartbeat reached another that still glowed, faintly. After a few taps, the screen reluctantly brought up the flickering images of another ship as it moved faster than the damaged screen could show.

The large display screen placed carefully up front and center of the disaster that was once a bridge showed the other ships between scattered lines of static and stars, then flickered and winked out as it failed completely. "Status?" Kiandra shouted as the crew turned and glared at her. "Okay, let me rephrase. What do we have left?"

"Kiandra?" Isaac said, looking back.

Kiandra's eyes focused on the boy's face. "Yes?"

"Can I ask you something?"

She shrugged. "I guess."

"You said you have a lot on your mind. Like what?"

Kiandra smiled. "You know, I don't think anyone has ever actually asked."

Isaac's eyes went wide. "Really? A pretty girl like you and no one ever wanted to know what you were thinking?"

"They might have wanted to know, but nope, no one never asked ... wait, you think I'm pretty?"

Isaac smiled. "Of course. From one to ten, I give you a twenty. No one ever told you that, either?"

"No."

"Then they are fools."

Kiandra's smile deepened. "Why don't you move back here with me. It will be easier for us to talk."

"You bet." Isaac looked at the bus driver, then flipped back to sit with Kiandra in one fluid motion. "I think we have our first class together too today. Writing composition is my favorite class."

Kiandra's eyes sparkled. "Really? It's my favorite too."

Everything is Relative

Rodger Brueger sat in his captain's chair on the bridge of the ISS *New Beginning*. His stomach knotted as they approached the target. For years they had been in stasis, hundreds in fact. But it was the only way. While fast, their drive wasn't originally intended to travel between the vast distances between stars.

He looked around at the empty, short backed, synth-leather seats on the cylindrical bridge, the rest of the crew were still in stasis. He didn't see the point in waking them unless this planet proved to have a viable future for them. The ISS *New Beginning* looked like a giant bullet crashing through space, packed with everything everyone thought they could use on the new world. Several decks held vehicles, others had fabrication equipment. One deck had a quick ready-made structure for them to live until the fabrication systems were online. And of course one deck they called the nursery held all the frozen fertilized eggs and incubation equipment waiting for the moment to begin rebuilding the human race.

Rodger blew out a breath he didn't know he was holding as he ran a finger around the collar of his itchy black uniform. Without anyone else awake, no one would know if he came up here in his underwear. But somehow it seemed right. And of course, Alex would tell the rest of the crew once they were awake. He was certain of that.

"Sir? We should reach local scanning range within the hour. Possibly as soon as twenty minutes," a voice came from the speaker above Rodger's head.

He looked up. "Thank you, Alex." While he would have preferred to fly the ship himself, the AI made it easier, not to mention more accurate. If he was off even the slightest amount, it could add decades or more to their journey. While they wouldn't notice it in stasis, the quicker they could arrive, the more power they would have for other uses down on the planet. He just hoped if the planet proved inhospitable, they could at least mine it for more fuel. Otherwise, it could be the end of the human race.

Rodger cringed at the thought. The end of the human race, who would have thought it could come so soon. Everyone assumed we had a many centuries or more before anything would drive us out of the solar system. First, something tore through Mars, destroying it, sending debris towards Earth and the ensuing gravitational changes started to move Earth out of its orbit as well. We were doomed unless we left. Thankfully, the *New Beginning* had already been under construction, although the design changed at that point.

Originally designed as a massive Martian transport to ferry goods and people between the planets, they repurposed it into humanity's last hope. To reduce the resources needed, stasis systems were installed. While untested for extreme periods, all the short-range tests had proven them viable. Rodger's eyes closed in a tight unseen grip as he thought about that. Sure, they were all still alive, but when he woke up, it felt like one-hundred ships had used his body as a landing strip. And oh, the taste in his mouth! He had never felt (or smelled) anything so foul.

He had been up several times during this trip, and each time he felt a little worse than the time before. He didn't relish the idea of going back into his popsicle-tube if this planet didn't turn out as they thought.

Rodger took a deep breath and wished he hadn't. The environmental system had been operational for only a few hours and still had hints of inactivity wafting through the air. It usually did a quick job of clearing the air once online, but every once in a while for a day or two, a pocket of something lingered. He never understood why it smelled like rotten cheese. Alex had run multiple diagnostics, but they always came up clean. He wished his nose did as well.

Touching a control on the arm of his chair, several holographic screens appeared surrounding him. He moved most of them out of the way, except for the main screen displaying the last sensor readings from the planet. Indications were water, and other necessary elements, but they couldn't be sure. They also couldn't tell if there were raging storms or if it was a tropical paradise at this distance.

Something caught his eye. He paused the image and tried to zoom in. He could have sworn he saw a tiny black dot for half a second. The displayed image contained a collage of exposures taken over the course of years. The image rewound backwards in time, then forwards. Rodger did this several times when he spotted the tiny black dot again. Something that had blocked a small area from the exposure. Rodger's one eyebrow went up. What could it be? He supposed it could be a natural effect, but his instincts said no.

He sat forward in his seat, trying to get a better look, to no avail, when a hand slithered around his back, making him jump. He turned to see Erica's Rambert's smiling face. His eyes went wide. She was still dressed in her white refridgerwear. At least that is what they called the one-piece white garment containing multiple sensors and monitors stitched into the fabric. Her long black hair hung down past her shoulders, and he tried to force his thoughts past her curves on display beneath the skin-tight fabric. "What are you doing up?"

Erica smiled before a stern look replaced the old. She put her hands on her hips. "That's some greeting. I set my tube so I could be here with you, and that is all you have to say?"

Rodger swallowed hard. When they had left Earth, they were simply colleagues, but now they were so much more. And of course, Erica being one of the last women in the universe. At least until they got the colony set up, and started the birthing of all the fertilized eggs they had stored in the lower decks. While there were three other women aboard, he had zero interest in them other than fellow crew members. He put on his best smile. "It's not that at all. I just didn't expect you. My first thought was of a malfunction. And what you heard was the voice of concern."

The lines on Erica's face softened and her eyes twinkled. Rodger loved that twinkle. She reached through the holographic screens again and took his right hand into hers. "In that case, I forgive you."

He pulled his hand back and pointed at the large holo screen in front, still displaying the planet. He waved a finger, and it zoomed a bit more, then pointed to the upper section. "Do you see anything unusual?"

She squinted and moved her eyes slowly from the top of the image to the bottom. She shook her head. "No, am I supposed to?"

Rodger waved a hand and touched several controls on the holoscreen as the image reversed, resumed, and reversed again in quick succession. "Anything now?"

Erica shook her head again. "No. Do you?"

Rodger sighed. "Watch the upper right quadrant as I play it slower." He adjusted the controls as Erica watched, squinting harder. "Anything now?"

"You mean that tiny black glitch in the image? Guess we need to check the telescope. Might be some damage."

Rodger rubbed the back of his neck as he sat back and deactivated the screens. "No, it can't be damage. If it was, the spot would be constant. But it disappears."

Erica gave a dismissive wave. "It just means there was some dirt or something and it cleared itself during the long exposure."

Rodger shook his head and enlarged the screen, pointing with his index finger at the black dot. "Look again. Dirt wouldn't move like this. Granted, it isn't much, but my instincts say it is something more."

She folded her arms and cocked her head towards the left as she turned to face him. "Like what?"

Rodger waved a hand again, deactivating the screens. "I don't know ... something." He leaned further back in his chair.

Erica moved behind the chair and started rubbing his neck, running her fingers over his shoulders and down, feeling the tight tendons. "You are wound tighter than an old spring. That little spot is bothering you that much?"

He sat up a bit and leaned into her fingers as she worked. "No, it's not that. Well, I suppose it is on some level. But the planet itself, what if it isn't what we need?"

She stopped, moved in front of him, and looked into his

eyes. "We still have enough fuel in the emergency reserve to make it to one more system if we need. You know that. It will take us longer, and it might be close, but we will get there."

Rodger sighed as he took her hands. "I know. Sorry, I should be more positive. I am the captain, after all."

Erica ran her fingers along the back of his knuckles as her eyes twinkled again. "Sweetheart, I know you would only tell me those worries. And if you can't tell me, who else are you going to tell? Hmm?"

A smile crept across his face as he looked up into her green eyes. "You have a point."

She took his hands in hers and squeezed. She ran her thumb over the back of index finger. "Of course I do."

Rodger wished he could take her back to their small quarters, but he knew now was not the time. "Alex? How much longer until we are close enough?"

"Five more minutes for an extreme range scan," came from the speaker over his head.

"Well then, I guess I had better take up my station." Erica released Rodger's hands and moved towards one console.

Rodger blinked. "Um, shouldn't you get dressed first?"

Erica sat in the chair of the nearest console to his right. "What? And miss this? Not on your life. Who is going to tell on me anyway? You?"

His heart sped up a notch at the thought. "I wouldn't dream of it. Besides, I am the captain. They would report it to me first. No way for them to find out, unless Alex blabs."

The speaker above his head clicked. "While I do not dream, the human expression 'I wouldn't dream of it' still applies." The speaker clicked off.

Erica giggled. "See?"

Rodger let out a slight grunt. "Yes." He ran his finger

down around the inside collar of his itchy uniform. Once again, wishing he hadn't worn it. But while Earth was gone, wearing it, he could almost pretend it still existed. He reactivated the holoscreens, and they surrounded him. He peeked over the one on his right at Erica, but she didn't see. Her eyes focused on her own console screens.

He turned back facing front to examine the image of the planet and its mysterious black spot. What was it? He ran the images back and forth several times. The spot still appeared and disappeared as before. But perhaps Erica was right, and the primary mirror of the telescope had a bit of debris that cleared out on its own over the long course of the exposure.

"We are now in local scanning range," Alex said a second before the speaker clicked off again. Rodger slid the image of the planet aside and brought up the raw data from the sensors. Several of the elements they needed, water being the most important, were available in abundance, as the previous indications suggested. But what caught his eye was the level of iron, carbon, and chromium were much higher than expected. Which made little sense. Either the planet had raging storms stirring up the atmosphere to an extreme level or ...

Rodger's eyes narrowed. "Alex, what do you make of these readings?"

"Sir, I do not 'make anything' from them. But while some levels are higher than we expected, it should make the planet more suitable for our needs." His speaker clicked off.

Erica folded her arms as she turned around in her chair. "What are you worried about now?"

He waved, and the surrounding screens flickered for a second before disappearing. "I'm not."

She glared. "I thought we settled this before? If can't tell me, who else?"

Rodger shifted in his seat, rising up on his right side as he angled his body away from her. Sometimes she could read him too well. "There is way too much iron, carbon, and chromium particles in the air."

Erica stood up, keeping her arms folded. "And you think it is because of raging storms down there?"

Rodger nodded, letting out a small sigh. "It is a strong possibility."

Erica took several steps forward and took his hands in hers again before going down on her haunches to look up into his brown eyes. "Sweetheart, we were just through this. If it is inhospitable, we can go on to the next. But from what I'm seeing, we still might be able to at least fill the tanks here, so we won't be stuck if the next one doesn't work out either."

Rodger squeezed her hands as he slid forward in his chair. He silently wished they had put more padding on the thing. For a captain's chair, it should have been a lot more comfortable. "Yes. I know. It just feels like we are missing something."

Her eyes narrowed further as she stood up. "I know that look. I also know you are more often than not, right in these cases."

The speaker above them clicked on. "Do you wish to abort the approach to the planet and target the secondary destination?"

Rodger shook his head. "Negative Alex, continue on course. We need more than my odd suspicions before I call an abort."

"Acknowledged." The speaker clicked off.

Erica glared as her grip on his hands tightened. "Okay, out with it. What is that look? What are you thinking?"

Rodger shook his head. Freed his hands from hers, reactivated the screens, extending their rotation point to encompass her as well, and pointed to the screen listing the elements in the atmosphere. "Look, that much in the atmosphere might mean storms yes, but it also could mean an alien civilization with decent technological advancements."

Erica moved closer to the one screen, looking at the information before turning a minute later with her hands on her hips. "You think aliens might be on this planet? From that small reading?"

"We are only on the very edge of scanning range. It could be the reason for the smallish amounts."

Erica shook her head. "Sweetheart, if it was an alien race with lots of technology, then we would be seeing a lot more, even at this distance."

Rodger leaned forward, arms on either side of the rests came together as his fingers made a steeple shape. "Or they are just getting started."

Erica's one eyebrow went up. "The start of their technological development?"

Rodger nodded. "Exactly. And means we can't use this planet's resources to fill our tanks if it's inhabited."

"Why not? They shouldn't mind. I mean, it isn't going to take much from them and certainly not anything they are going to miss." She moved back over and sat in her chair, turning it in a slow sway back and forth.

Rodger dropped his hands, then waved the screens away. "No. It is possible we would influence them or cause large social problems with our appearance."

Erica raised one shoulder and let it fall. "If they see us. If they aren't significantly advanced, we could slip down there, get what we need, and take off again before they would ever know. They won't miss the little water we would take to process into deuterium."

Rodger sighed. "They might not miss it. But is it right?"

The speaker above clicked on. "Do you wish to abort the approach to the planet and alter course to the secondary location?"

Rodger ran his fingers through his hair. "I don't know Alex."

Erica's eyes narrowed. "Look, you know as well I, we and this ship are humanity's last hope of survival. They won't miss a little water. But I say wait until we get closer to see if these readings are correct. And if there are any other surprises. We can still head off to alternate system at any point if we have to."

He sat back and looked up at the ceiling. "True. Alex, remain on course and continue scanning. Alert us to any changes."

"Acknowledged." The speaker clicked off.

Erica started heading towards the hatch at the back of the bridge behind Rodger. He turned, his chair rotating on its pivot point. "Where are you going?"

She turned, looking over her shoulder. "Well, it looks like we aren't going to know anything for a while, and I figured I would get changed. Got to get dressed sometime." She stuck out one bare foot behind her and wiggled her toes. "Besides, these deck plates are cold."

"And here I thought you might want my help."

Erica turned, looking back towards him out of the corner of her eye. The gleam had returned, along with a playful smile. "Not now. Perhaps later." She disappeared through the hatch before he could say anything more.

* * *

Rodger continued walking down the corridor on deck six. Rows and rows of oblong incubation equipment, with their rounded center area, sat on the right side. While on the left, freezers were stacked sometimes three high with hundreds of fertilized eggs per unit. A chill ran down his spine as he checked the status of each unit. They kept this area cooler than the rest of the ship, even when the crew was awake. No one was down here much.

But Rodger liked to check over everything. Captains always inspected their ships. And they couldn't afford any failures in here. Although Alex should know the instant any freezer or system registered as less than optimal, unless the problem was in his connection to them. He trusted nothing entirely on its own. While Alex had proven himself time and time again, anything could malfunction.

He heard a buzz on a nearby com, and he touched the panel. It lit up, and he heard Alex's voice. "Sir, we are close enough for a more detailed scan. I have done so, and there are differences."

Rodger grimaced as he chewed his upper lip. "Better or worse?"

"I cannot determine that. The concentrations of iron and carbon elements have increased."

"Anything more?"

"Nothing that I can detect. However, we are still moving at relative speed, affecting scanning capabilities. Do you wish to abort?" Alex said in his normal monotone voice.

Rodger thought about it. They would save some fuel if they aborted now, but the amount wouldn't make that much difference when traveling to the secondary location.

"Negative. We might as well get a good look at the place before we take off again. Begin final deceleration and sling shot us into a high orbit."

"Acknowledged. Beginning final deceleration. We will come out of relative speed in one day five hours and achieve orbit fifteen hours after that."

Rodger straightened. This was faster than he expected. "Excellent. Where is Erica?"

"She left the bridge two minutes ago en route to the galley," Alex said.

Rodger let a grin spread across his face. They hadn't had breakfast together in a long time, relatively speaking. "Thank you Alex, I will catch her there. But don't tell her I'm coming."

"You are welcome sir, and acknowledged." The com panel went dark.

Rodger walked to the end of the corridor, entered the elevator, and tapped the control for the crew area. A few seconds later, he stepped out onto the crew deck and made his way to the end of the corridor and to the galley. The hatch sat in its open position, and he poked his head in to smell the aroma of bacon and eggs. "Mmm, that smells good."

Erica jumped and turned around. "I thought you were down below doing a check on the nursery?"

Rodger smiled. Erica hadn't put on her uniform. Instead, she had opted for a pair of tight green pants with a matching shirt. More comfortable, but left little to the imagination. "I finished. Alex told me you were up here and I thought we might have breakfast together."

Erica frowned and put her hands on her hips. "You still haven't eaten yet? You were up long before me."

Rodger grinned. "Yes, well, I had a lot to do this morning."

Erica folded her arms. She swore the guy would die of starvation if she wasn't around. "Alex does a lot. Let him do it while you eat. He doesn't have to." She placed a second packet of food in the oven. A needle entered a corner of the package, injected a precise amount of water, and began heating the entire package. "I wasn't expecting you, so give me a minute while yours cooks."

Rodger moved over to the one small table on the left side of the galley and slid into a seat. "Of course. And I could have made it. I didn't mean you had to make mine before you could eat."

"I don't mind, really. Besides, it is easy. I don't do much other than punch in what is being made, and the oven does the rest." She held up her opened packet of bacon and eggs. "Hundreds of years old and it's still good."

Rodger sighed. "Yeah, makes you wonder what all they did to it."

The oven beeped, and she pulled out the other packet, opened it onto a tray and handed it to Rodger. "Well, they preserved us okay, so I figure it can't be that bad since we are still alive."

Rodger shoved a fork full of reconstituted eggs into his mouth and tried not to think how old they were. But now it proved impossible. He swallowed hard. "What a thought."

Erica handed him a pouch filled with dark liquid. "Here, the coffee will help it go down." She slid into the seat opposite of him.

Rodger took the pouch and took a sip. Then another. He never could resist coffee. He decided on trying to focus his mind on something else rather than breakfast. "Alex told me there were increases in iron and carbon in the atmosphere."

He shoved another fork full of eggs into his mouth, this time without thinking about it, and swallowed without issue.

Erica took a bite of her eggs. "Oh? That must have just happened. He didn't mention it to me."

Rodger put the last fork-full of eggs into his mouth and chewed on a strip of bacon before washing it down with the coffee. "It did. But I decided the fuel savings are negligible with an abort at this point. And the civilization we appear to be approaching won't be able to see us, anyway. Might as well get a good look at them before we take off again."

Erica sat up straighter. "And fill up the tanks?"

Rodger shook his head. "I doubt it. Depends. If we can find an area that is uninhabited and no one can detect our approach, perhaps."

"Should we wake the rest of the crew?"

He shook his head again. "No, no point in that until we know for sure. We might be heading right back out again."

Erica took the last bite of her breakfast and washed it down with her own pouch of coffee. "So when do we arrive?"

"I'm going to double check Alex, but we should come out of relative speed in one day five hours. And we should be in orbit fifteen hours after that."

"Wonderful. You go do that and I will be waiting in our quarters for you to finish."

Rodger's head popped up. "What? But ..."

"I said later. And this is later. Not to mention we have a day to kill."

"But–"

"Listen, you already finished the inspections, right?"

Rodger thought about all they had to do. But she was right, with the inspections done, everything working properly, and Alex flying the ship, they did have a little time. "Yes, I did."

"Good. Then it's settled. Unless you don't want to see me in something very different."

His heart skipped a beat. "No, no, not at all." He stood up and started backing towards the hatch with the goofiest grin on his face. "I'll do that and meet up with you shortly." He disappeared behind the hatch door.

"Don't be too long," she called after him. But she knew he wouldn't be. Men were so easy at times.

* * *

Rodger sat in his captain's chair on the bridge of the ISS *New Beginning* back in his uniform. While he hadn't worn it for almost the past day, now it felt it appropriate. Erica sat at her console to his right in a pair of black stretch pants and a simple green shirt with a scooped neck. She offered to put on her uniform as well, but he said there wasn't a reason for them to both be uncomfortable. She had frowned, and they discussed it at length. But in the end she went with comfort rather than appearance.

Rodger took a deep breath and was relieved the environmental system had finally cleared all the strange scents from the last period of inactivity. And the horrible taste in his mouth had disappeared as well. Although Erica might have had more to do with that.

The scanners had shown steady increases in iron and carbon in the atmosphere. But nothing unusual for a civilization in the early stages of technological development. While Erica remained skeptical, Rodger remained certain.

The speaker in the ceiling clicked. "Final transition out of relative speed in ten seconds. Prepare yourselves," Alex said.

Erica grabbed her chair with one hand and her console with

the other. Remembering the last time they did this. The ISS *New Beginning* began vibrating as she decelerated below the threshold of relative speed. The vibrations increased and caused Rodger to grip the sides of his chair harder.

They increased again and Rodger began to wonder if the ship was going to shake apart when, as quick as it started, it stopped. "We have come out of relative speed, all systems are functional. Scanners reporting additional data. Relaying to your consoles," Alex said.

Rodger brought up his holoscreens and the image of the planet appeared on the large central screen. But it had changed. Along the side of planet's image scrolled the elements in the atmosphere along with general composition. He blinked. This wasn't possible. The numbers had gone up exponentially. And they were heading towards the planet's night side and sections of it appeared lit up. "What in the world?"

Erica laughed. "Quite accurate. It would appear our aliens developed a lot faster than we thought. But looks like you were right, sweetheart."

Rodger sighed. "I wish I wasn't. But this makes little sense. A developing civilization shouldn't be able to jump ahead technologically that fast. Granted, we were at relative speed during our last readings, so it was very possible they were looking into the past between those readings and these. But still, in that short period of time, they couldn't have gone from being on the edge to this."

Erica stood up and moved over next to him. "But they did." She watched as the image of the planet changed with the coming of dawn. Is there any way we can still sneak down there¿'

Rodger shook his head. "No. They are all over the planet.

In fact, I'm worried they might spot our approach."

Erica turned to face him. "You think they have advanced that far?"

He pointed to the image of the planet. "Look at that and you tell me? They obviously have power and large numbers. Anything is possible. Alex, do we have sufficient speed to do an abort now?"

"Affirmative. However, it will take a good portion of our reserve fuel," Alex said.

Rodger's head hung down as he ran his fingers through his dark hair. "I was afraid of that. We are committed now. At least to orbit their planet several times before we can execute a gravity assist maneuver. Otherwise, we will never make it to another system. I just hope they don't see us."

The speaker above clicked. "Sir, I am detecting a transmission."

Rodger sighed, lowered his head, and pivoted it left and right. "Too late."

Erica put her hand on his shoulder. "Wait. It may not be aimed at us. It could be something beamed in all directions. You know the amount of junk transmissions we sent into space for almost a century."

"True." He slid the image of the planet to the side and brought up a new holoscreen displaying a sine-wave. The composition felt strangely familiar. "Alex? Can you make anything out of this?"

"Yes, it is similar to our com frequencies but with several changes along the power utilization curve. I am altering our equipment to compensate."

A few moments later, the image of the sine-wave gave way to a screen full of flashing black and white static. The static shifted in form and variance until it ultimately gave way to the image of a human face with salt and pepper hair, brown eyes and a broad face with deep lines. Rodger's eyes went wide as Erica's jaw dropped. "ISS *New Beginning*, do you receive us? Please acknowledge this transmission."

Rodger turned. "What do you think? Could this be a trick of some sort?"

Erica shook her head. "I don't think so. The guy looks human enough, and is even wearing a uniform. It is a lot different from ours, but has several similarities, too."

"Could be a hologram," Rodger said.

"I suppose, but might as well say something. I mean, they know we are here."

"ISS *New Beginning*, Are you operational? Captain Rodger Brueger, please respond to this transmission."

This time, Erica's eyes went wide as her head jerked back. "Can't be a trick. How would they know your name?"

"But how can this be possible? Earth was destroyed. We were the only ship to escape."

"Do you wish me to respond?" Alex said.

Rodger sighed. "Can't do any harm at this point. Yes, and activate the visual as well."

The face on the screen smiled. "Captain Brueger, it is good to see your ship is still operational. I am Commander Hilson. While we detected your ship some time ago, we were unable to contact you until the *New Beginning* came out of relative speed. Which was a great relief, I can tell you. Many here on New Hope for the last couple hundred years or so thought the systems had malfunctioned and the *New Beginning* was a bullet heading to split our planet."

Rodger blinked in slow motion. "Couple ... of ... hundred ... years?"

"Yes, although we have been expecting you for a lot longer

than that. A thousand years at least." The camera angle changed, showing more of Commander Hilson and the staff working behind him at various consoles. All of them wore black uniforms similar to his. "No doubt you are wondering what happened. There will be time for a full debriefing later, but in summary, right after you left, we developed a new kind of dimensional drive allowing humanity to travel between stars in days rather than many years. Earth was growing cold due to the gravitational shifts, but other advancements slowed down its cooling giving us more time. In the end, we managed to build several new ships before it was too late and take off for other systems. New Hope is the latest system we have colonized."

"We survived?" Erica said.

Commander Hilson smiled as he sat up straighter in his chair. "Not only survived, but thrived. The human race has colonized fifty systems and continuing to expand. I will upload all the data to your AI. We look forward to your arrival. Welcome to New Hope." His image flickered slightly before it vanished.

Erica frowned as she folded her arms. "What I don't get is how is this possible? It has only been a couple of hundred years since we left Earth."

"Due to our traveling near the speed of light, while what happened on Earth might only be two hundred years for us, has been thousands for them," Alex said.

Rodger sat back in his chair and slouched down a bit. His mission had been for nothing, but at least they hadn't forgotten about them in the multiple millenniums since they left. He let out a deep sigh, looking up at Erica. "Relatively speaking, of course."

About The Author

Don is the author of eight science fiction novels and many more short stories. He lives in the USA where he continues to dream up more fantastic worlds for you to enjoy. When not writing, he can usually be found devouring another science fiction book, TV series, or movie.

Other works by Don DeBon:

The Husband

Erin's Husband is not himself.

Her Husband acts different and Erin will find out why.

One night Jack returns from a walk in the woods a changed man. He walks like him, talks like him, yet very different ... more romantic than ever.

With a suspicious eye, Erin watches. And what she learns could have dire consequences for the entire human race.

Love a good romance with a Science Fiction twist? Grab The Husband today!

Red Warp

Red, a woman with an amazing gift, the gift of passing though time and space without the need of any bulky equipment.

Captured and held in an integration room, she must escape. The only way she can.

Now blasted off course, running for her life with the FBI for company.

Red Warp a fun romp through time with twists and turns to keep you guessing right until the end.

Time Rock

Professor Keleeigan sat over one of his consoles in his adapted lab tweaking several wave guides on the display. He felt a slight shiver as the temperature started to drop. He brushed a loch of white hair behind his ear as rolled his chair over the ancient wood floor and picked up a tiny chip no larger than his fingernail. Fresh solder fumes wafted up his nose as he installed it within one of the open systems on the table. The status lights on the side continued to flash orange.

When the lights finally turn green, everything seemed ready.

Trisia wearing her best heels and matching dress for a night of fun, now stuck with a foolish old man instead.

Time travel. It never goes as planned.

Amazon USA
http://www.amazon.com/

Goodreads
http://www.goodreads.com

Connect with the Author
Email: writer.don.debon@gmail.com
Mailing List: http://eepurl.com/bxWAov
Website: http://www.dondebon.com
Twitter: @DonDeBon

This Edition Published 2022 by
DBDigital Publishing

ISBN 978-1-948819-11-4
ISBN 978-1-948819-10-7 **(e-book)**

Cat Trouble ©2022
Scared Stiff ©2022
Lisa ©2018
The Run ©2018
The Storm ©2017
The Transport ©2016
Everything is Relative ©2022